Beth licked her lips

Spencer James at his best wasn't nice. When experiencing the throes of lust, he was a man possessed.

He yanked her against him and his mouth ripped into hers, showing her how madly he wanted to make love to her.

God save him, she was just as wild.

Some time in the next few hours, she would be running back to that putz of a date, but right now she was Spencer's and he wasn't about to let her walk.

His mouth fed on her, her neck, the sexy spot below her ear. Every inch needed to be touched, caressed.

By him.

And at that moment he could have shot to the moon with all the compressed power inside him. He had to have her, find the secret key that unlocked the pleasure within her. Tonight he'd discover it all.

Dear Reader,

I have to confess that Spencer holds a special place in my heart. I knew that I would have to write a unique hero for Beth. She was lonely, wanted to find love, and for all intents and purposes should have found a nice guy to settle down with in the burbs. But she didn't. Leave it to Beth to do things the hard way. From the moment she met Spencer, she knew he was the one. He was arrogant, brusque, intelligent and clueless about women. And ladies, that's one seriously sexy combination.

I hope you enjoy reading Beth's story. Next month brings THE BACHELORETTE PACT to a close with Cassandra's story. Write to me at P.O. Box 312, Nyack, NY 10960, and let me know what you think.

Kathleen O'Reilly

Books by Kathleen O'Reilly

HARLEQUIN TEMPTATION
889—JUST KISS ME
927—ONCE UPON A MATTRESS
967—PILLOW TALK*
971—IT SHOULD HAPPEN TO YOU*

HARLEQUIN DUETS
66—A CHRISTMAS CAROL

*The Bachelorette Pact

KATHLEEN O'REILLY

BREAKFAST AT BETHANY'S

HARLEQUIN®

TORONTO • NEW YORK • LONDON
AMSTERDAM • PARIS • SYDNEY • HAMBURG
STOCKHOLM • ATHENS • TOKYO • MILAN • MADRID
PRAGUE • WARSAW • BUDAPEST • AUCKLAND

To that special group of loopy ladies
who make me laugh and cry, and remind me on a daily basis
about the joy of being a writer.

ISBN 0-373-69175-0

BREAKFAST AT BETHANY'S

Copyright © 2004 by Kathleen Panov.

This edition published by arrangement with Harlequin Books S.A.

® and TM are trademarks of the publisher. Trademarks indicated with
® are registered in the United States Patent and Trademark Office, the
Canadian Trade Marks Office and in other countries.

www.eHarlequin.com

Printed in U.S.A.

1

SWF looking to meet good man. Must like romantic walks, fine wine and old movies. Geeks need not apply.

BETH VON MEETER WAS THE last one to leave the chapel. Weddings did that to her. For some people it was sloppy puppies, for her it was the magic of the whole bridal extravaganza.

Wistfully, she trailed her fingers over the cute little nosegays that were tied to the pews. She would have chosen daisies rather than roses if it were her day.

But it wasn't.

Beth would have opted for a storybook June wedding rather than a cold November day, but then Mickey had no patience for social obligations, and well, to be frank, she and Dominic were in a hurry.

Mickey's wedding ceremony had been small—pitifully small. The reception at the church afterward had been almost nonexistent. Of course, that was the best you could do when the groom had to keep his name under wraps. Top secret, hush-hush. I Married a Mafia Don: My Love Affair with the Mob.

A gorgeous, sensitive, undercover cop wiseguy. It was enough to make a girl fall on her knees, rail and shake a fist at the sky. "As God is my witness, I'll never be single again." Unfortunately, imaginary drama wouldn't do diddly to conjure up the perfect life.

Carefully she smoothed out the pale pink material of her bridesmaid dress. That made two bridesmaid dresses that were flying in her closet at half-mast. Oh, yeah, the Bachelorette Pact. Single forever! Long live the infinite torture of the dating ritual! Beth blew a raspberry, which she hoped wasn't sacrilegious, but she figured God would understand. God wasn't married, either.

Now Mickey was. And Jessica was. Beth wasn't.

"Forget something?" asked Cassandra, gliding into the chapel. Amazing. The woman oozed sexuality even on holy ground.

Beth took in one last sniff of the roses. "Not a thing." Then she bundled up in her coat and slung her bag over her shoulder in what she thought was a sassy move. "Are Jessica and Adam still here? We could get a drink," she suggested, hoping no one would actually take her up on it. She felt like the worst sort of party squasher. Possibly it was her sinuses. She was grasping at straws, but tonight she just wasn't feeling perky.

Cassandra picked up one of the nosegays and

lightly traced a rose petal with her forefinger. "We could if you want. I thought you had a date."

"I have one scheduled for 9:45 p.m." Beth checked her watch. Two hours to liftoff. So far, she'd been on eleven dates with her Internet dating service. Yes, you heard that right folks, eleven. It was demoralizing, dehumanizing and downright depressing.

"Have you met your match?" asked Cassandra, sitting down on an old oak bench and looking as if she were actually interested.

That made Beth sit down, too. "I've been on eleven dates and I think I've found the dregs of the dating pool."

"That bad?"

"I've met Viktor the eccentric—read 'mad'—Russian. Kyle, who's exploring his more feminine side. That man is going to need luck with cross-gender dating, because his feminine side is pretty pronounced."

"Poor baby," murmured Cassandra.

Beth waved her hand. "Oh, that's not all. We have Bob, who likes to eat—a lot, not that there's anything wrong with that. The painfully, and I do mean painfully, shy Ted. Bob II, whose favorite topic of conversation is himself. Blah, blah, blah, Bob this. Blah, blah, blah, Bob that." She wrapped her head in her hands. "It's a nightmare."

"Maybe you'll find more promising candidates."

"Those *are* the most promising candidates."

She was spared further depression when an elderly janitor opened the creaky door into the chapel, the cold wind cutting through the last of the heat. "I'm locking up for the night. You girls need to clear out of here."

Beth stood and looked at the remaining flowers, then shot a what-the-hell? glance at Cassandra. "Are you going to throw these out?"

The janitor winked at Beth and stuffed his hands into his coat pockets. For a moment she wished he were about fifty years younger, or even forty. "You're welcome to take some home. I used to bring the leftovers to my wife when she was alive."

Quickly Beth tucked a nosegay inside her purse. "Thank you. I'll give them a good home."

Cassandra was already walking out the door ahead of her, but just before the janitor shut them out, she whisked back in, wrinkling her nose. "Maybe just one."

Beth just smiled. For all her big talk, Cassandra looked to be just as jealous as the rest of single America. Even a great sex life didn't remove the lonely truth when you went home alone. Vindication was sweet.

SPENCER JAMES WASN'T USED to being kept waiting. He liked punctuality, he liked schedules, he liked organization. His ex-wife had called him anal. Thoughts of his ex sent his fingers tapping impatiently on the linen tablecloth. He preferred the term "driven," which was more precise. A reporter lived and died by his adjectives.

The waiter came by, and Spencer shook his head. Annoying toady. Then he checked his watch, but it'd only been thirty seconds since the last time he'd looked.

Finally he took out his notebook and began to jot down some ideas for his piece. Humiliating. Soft news. As the result of a misguided bet—Spencer had said the Cubs would win the pennant—he was now working in Tempo, that is, the lifestyle section. Fashion, gossip and food. Fluff.

It wouldn't earn him a Scripps-Howard Award like the article he'd done on corruption in the Chicago unions, but his editor seemed to think the feature profile on the age of Internet dating would be picked up by the AP.

The impersonality of the personal ad. Not just for the lovelorn, it was now part of the mainstream. Singles didn't congregate in bars like packs of blathering hyenas, they sat alone in their bedrooms instead, with just the dim light of the computer screen to keep them warm. In short, it was a lot like his own life.

Lost in his thoughts, he found the words began to flow. When the hostess arrived at the table, he almost told her off—until he saw the ash blonde standing next to her.

Pretty, somewhat shy, but with an innocence in her blue eyes. Ingenue—not that he believed in them anymore. They'd gone the way of the dodo, but still there was an artlessness and honesty there that made her unique.

The perfect subject. Inspiration sent his pulse racing. How hard could it be to convince her to let him write about all the excruciatingly painful details of her love life?

Then he stood up and held out his hand in a businesslike manner. She smiled back at him, an open expression in the cerulean eyes.

Absolutely perfect.

SPENCER JAMES WASN'T QUITE the SWM she'd been expecting. Age? He looked to be thirtyish, not the fifty-two-year-old that seemed more likely. Hair substance? Not balding. His blond locks looked inviting and thick, the streaks of brown giving it just the right touch to spoil the pretty-boy image. Much dishevelment potential there.

When he'd stood up, she'd gotten an eyeful of the bod. Muscles. Height. No paunch or spare tire visible. Good clothes sense. Black open-necked shirt and slacks. Casual, elegant.

After the waiter brought their drinks, Spencer started on the pre-dinner conversation. Refreshingly enough, he didn't waste time with small talk, he simply began asking her questions. At first it was jolting, the way he fired them like a sharpshooter, but then she relaxed and began to enjoy herself. He didn't seem to worry about pretenses or social niceties, he merely seemed curious, asking her multitudes of things, most pertaining to the dating process.

A newbie, she thought to herself. And so she did her best to educate him.

When he took a sip of wine, she took advantage of the momentary lapse to ask him some questions of her own.

"Do you live with your family?" she asked, wondering what his issues were. Every man that she'd met so far had issues, and this man in front of her was just too, too perfect.

He shook his head, looking puzzled. "No. Patricide is frowned on in our family."

What an odd sense of humor. Only the tiny crinkles in the corners of his eyes gave him away.

"So, Spencer James, what do you do with your daytime hours?" Mentally she rolled her eyes. She'd be asking his sign next. So far she was enjoying herself too much, and the lust factor was running off the charts.

There had to be a catch.

"I'm a journalist," he said, his fingers twisting on

the wineglass. "In fact, I'm working on a story right now."

Beth nodded politely, and reminded herself to keep quiet about the sixteen articles she'd sold to *True Fantasies.* She picked up her glass of chardonnay—according to the weight guide, 2 points—and gave him an "isn't-that-nice?" smile.

"I was wondering if you'd be willing to help?" he asked, his eyes sharper now. The smoky-gray was metamorphing into granite. Solid granite, not that faux stuff you found on countertops.

"I actually don't know what I could possibly do to help," she began.

But he cut her off. "Internet dating. I want to follow a subject through the bits and bytes of finding a mate via computer. It's fascinating and the public would love to read about it."

The lightbulb flashed and her heart sank into her toes. So there was a crack in his facade, after all. This was one big research project for him. He was probably married. "You're not even single, are you?" she asked sadly.

"Actually, I am. But I'm not interested in experiencing the process myself. I really just want to write about it. Ascertain if Internet dating is used because of the lack of free time to investigate more accepted means, or if it's still the modus of last resort."

"You just want to study us poor, pitiful schmiels

who are forced into it?" she said, blinking her eyelashes innocently.

"Exactly." Then he grimaced, with a foot-in-mouth expression. Beth was cheered by that bit of token humanness. He seemed so detached about everything else.

"No, not exactly," he corrected, but then he leaned in, all conspiratorial-like. "But I want to be candid with you. I want to know if the schmiel-factor is still there."

Beth started to gather her things, feeling the blush high on her cheeks. "I'm not the right candidate for you."

He stopped her with a hand to her arm. "You're the perfect candidate."

That was *soooo exactly* the wrong thing to say. Camel straws, dam stoppage, end-of-the-ropeness. She was no longer going to be stepped on and smile prettily about it.

She was going to grow teeth. No, *fangs.* Fangs were even deadlier. Beth smiled at him and tossed her head. "What do I get out of this?" *Oh, that was good.*

"I could pay you."

Not enough, buckaroo. Not for a zillion dollars. "No, thank you." She swung her purse onto her shoulder, narrowly missing his eye. Beth had great purse aim. He was just lucky she wasn't really ticked off.

"I could help you," he said, a hint of charm in his voice.

Now that was more interesting. She stopped. Her eyes wandered over him as if he were a six-foot Hershey bar. "How?" she asked, quirking a brow. Actually, quirking two, because she couldn't do one yet.

"You want to meet men, right?"

She narrowed her eyes and nodded.

"Your ad needs revising. I can do that."

"What's wrong with my ad?"

"It's not vibrant enough. You need to add some punch, some color."

Her newly installed gullibility meter started beeping. "How do you know about ads? I thought you were above computer dating?"

He shrugged, calling attention to his well-defined chest muscles. He probably didn't even have to exercise. She was really starting to hate this guy. "I've done my research for the story. Words are my life," he answered. "What do you say?"

"I want a guarantee."

"What do you mean?" he asked, because obviously he didn't live in her new, improved, tough-as-nails world.

"I want dates from this. Great dates. Or the deal's off." Then she leaned on the table, letting the candlelight reflect favorably on her cheekbones. All in all, it was a great moment. "Besides, that's what you want, isn't it? To prove that computer dating isn't for losers?" *Like me,* she almost added. "That's not interesting. You want to write something ground-breaking. An evolution in the courtship ritual. Maybe coin a new word for the dictionary."

A less refined man would be drooling, but even Mr. Savoir Faire couldn't hide the excitement in his eyes. "I'll get you great dates. If I can't write a good singles ad, then I'm in the wrong business."

Success. The night was looking up. Beth sat down, satisfied with her negotiation skills. Not bad for a beginner. Of course, you should never underesti-mate a Von Meeter when it came to negotiation.

"Where do you want to start?" she asked, sipping her wine with a little more gusto. Maybe even choc-olate mousse later—eight points. She'd never or-dered dessert on a date before, but he wanted hon-esty. Food honesty was the most basic of all, except for sexual honesty, which was pretty much nonex-istent.

He placed his tape recorder on the table, a little digital thingamabob. "I'm going to tape the conver-sation, but I want to make some notes while we talk. We'll start with the simple things. Tell me about yourself."

"I work at Java4U," she said defensively, just wanting to get that out in the open.

"Lack of education or motivation?"

"Neither," she said, her hands starting to get nervous. She didn't like these what-are-you-doing-with-your-life? conversations, for obvious reasons. "I like people," she added, which was her standard answer.

"Very decent of you, but there are better opportunities out there for people who like people."

"You don't like people, do you?" she asked, neatly switching the subject from her career or lack thereof.

He cleared his throat and smiled with effort. "Why don't we talk about something else? When did you decide to try computer dating? Do you have friends who have done this?"

At first it was difficult, but he coaxed her into more. His reporter voice was calm and soothing. Trust-inducing. Very smooth. And so over dinner, she found herself responding, relaxing, and she began to talk.

To vent, really. To explain in great, cathartic details about all the problems with the current singleton environment.

As the waiter cleared away the last of the dishes, she started in on the biggest problem.

"I never had trouble until my friends started getting married. Now we don't hang out together, and I'm like this old piece of clothing that just doesn't fit anymore. They look at me and don't know what to do. I was the favorite shirt, but now I've got stains that won't come out, and it's not like anyone is going to wear me anymore. Instead I sit hidden away in the back of their closet. It sucks. Do you still have single friends?"

He paused in his writing and looked up. "No. They're all married."

"How do you go out, then? How do you meet women?"

His pen started tapping on the table. "I don't."

Then she noticed the black shirt, the innate sense of style, the perfect abs. God, all the signs were there. "Oh."

The pen hit the table. "What does that mean?" he said, the smoothness gone from his voice.

She buried her fingers in her napkin. How embarrassing. "I'm not going to make judgments on anyone's personal life."

He smiled tightly, his hands clenched together in pre-strangulation mode. "I like women. I love women. I was married to a woman."

He did have that been-there, done-that air about him. "Didn't work out?" she pried, because she understood completely.

"It lasted eighteen months. Seventeen of which were hell."

"Mine lasted two weeks," she admitted. She had eloped with Kenny when she was a freshman in college. She had thought it was romantic to marry a musician. *Quelle horreur.*

"You were lucky," he said, and she noticed his hands had stopped clenching.

"You sound bitter."

"I have a right to be," he said, picking up the pen once more. His own little shield.

"Want to talk about it?" Beth asked.

"No." The pen was back to scribbling. "Tell me about the perfect man. Most important quality."

And that was all for the personal life. Back to business. "He's got to be smart. Brains are very important to me."

Spencer looked up, laying the pen on the table. "What about looks? There are lots of smart, homely guys. In fact, you put that in your ad and you'll be married in approximately three to seven days."

She shook her finger at him. A man should never assume. "I said intelligence was important. You didn't ask what the number two thing was."

"So looks are number two?"

Those assumptions were really going to bite him in the butt. And he'd said he was a journalist. "No. A sense of humor is number two."

He continued to scribble on the paper. She tried to peek, but his writing was illegible.

"Looks are number three?" he asked, without looking up.

"No. He needs to have depth. I can't stand those shallow men that only tell you what you want to hear."

The pen drooped. He met her eyes. "But don't you think computer dating is in and of itself shallow?" He struggled for words. "The process sucks all the humanity out of that first spark of meeting. It's premeditated."

He was a closet romantic: How I Unearthed my Lover's Secrets. Fascinated, she balanced her elbows on the table and studied him. "But you're a journalist. You of all people should know that words can be more seductive than the visual."

That made him laugh. "I've never gotten off from reading."

"I have," said Beth, suddenly quite pleased with herself. Now who was the schmiel?

Mr. Hotshot Journalist-Man was rendered speechless. His face turned primitive—eyes narrowed, nostrils flaring, breathing shallow. All facts seemed to indicate that Mr. James was seeing her as a sexual being, not just a guinea pig.

She would have been lying if she didn't admit to feeling a little squishy herself—okay, a lot.

There were many reasons why she wanted to shock him. Some of it was the simple biological response to the highly charged testosterone that was shooting from every solid inch of him.

But there was more to it than just chemistry. She'd always felt like a bystander in life, not the ambitious one, not the intelligent one, not the sexy one. She'd skirted along, moving from job to job, boyfriend to boyfriend, not ever needing to settle.

She'd never seen anything wrong with that until now. Now, as he stared at her with those cool gray eyes that made him just as much a bystander as she was, she got mad.

He thought her love life was great fodder for his article, and nothing else.

She met his eyes squarely, with a show of bravado she'd never attempted before. This time she wasn't about to look away.

He glanced down at his paper, his cheeks flushed, but he wasn't writing.

She'd made him stop writing.

It was a small victory, but a victory nonetheless.

SPENCER CLOSED HIS EYES and began to count. He was a professional. He just needed to concentrate on something other than the far too appealing fantasy of the woman across from him playing under her skirts while reading *Cosmo.*

Slowly, the fog lifted and he opened his eyes. Still she was watching him. Some part of him, the non-glandular part, wanted to forget the whole incident and concentrate on the issues at hand, namely his story. Spence had learned a long time ago how to turn off the female of the species. He'd turned into a first-class asshole. A drastic measure, but effective. Besides, the reputation had helped his career.

Tonight, though, the more ruling part of him, namely his erection, felt a response was in order. A physical response. Already he was anticipating that physical response. She wanted to play games?

He lifted his glass to her. "Salute. To the pursuit of pleasure."

She lifted her glass to her lips, eyeing him over the crystal edge. There was some uncertainty in her face, but the blue eyes were dark with knowledge.

"I shouldn't have strayed," she murmured. "Let's get back to the matter at hand. After all, this is being recorded for posterity."

"Not for posterity," he corrected. "Just for my own personal review."

"Still, I'm babbling."

"No, my dear. You're seducing me, and that's an entirely different matter."

BETH FELT HER blood pressure rising to near volcanic proportions. The pig. The arrogant swine. As if she'd like to bed him. *Of course she would.*

As if she'd like to see if he could kiss as well as he could talk. *Mais certainement!*

His gray eyes were daring her to continue. *Go ahead, missy, do me.*

Beth smiled grimly. "Let's stick to business, shall we?"

"If you insist."

She glared. "I insist. You've said you can get me

great dates. However, I think we need to define the terminology we'll be using. Great for me indicates a man who is handsome—"

"Aha! Looks are important."

Her knife was calling to her. "Intelligent," she grated out between clenched teeth. "Sensitive. And not a boor."

"Then you'll have to change things around." He pulled a folder from his briefcase. "Instead of saying 'Looking to meet good man' say 'Are you worthy?' It implies you're confident and above clichés."

"'Looking to meet good man' is not a cliché."

"It's the most cliché of clichés."

Beth threw her napkin over her knife, just to eliminate temptation. "Let's move on."

"Romantic walks." He shook his head. "It means you're fat."

The napkin came off the knife. A knife that had cut through approximately twenty-seven Weight Watchers points' worth of food. "I'm not fat."

"No, but a man will read between the lines. It implies that you don't want to do anything to break a sweat. Including having sex. No wonder you're having problems here."

"I understand," she said, suddenly comprehending why his wife had divorced him.

"The 'good wine' bit isn't bad."

"Thank you for that vote of confidence."

He continued on, ignoring her. "If you'd said

martinis or cosmopolitans, you might get a livelier crowd. Just as long as you don't mention beer."

"Why?"

"Beer means you're fat."

"I hate beer."

He looked her over. "And it shows."

Quickly she changed the subject. "Old movies? I suppose I should say action movies, right?"

"No, the average single man will read 'old movies' and think that he can put up with it, and then get laid on the couch. Old movies are a great aphrodisiac."

"Do *you* think old movies are a great aphrodisiac?" she asked, suddenly curious.

He frowned for a moment, as if he'd never considered the idea of aphrodisiacs. "No."

She folded her hands together gracefully, the image of calm. "Ah, but you're not the average single man."

"God forbid."

She polished off the last of her wine. No dessert tonight. It was getting late, and she was feeling fat. "So how would you rewrite my ad?"

He looked up in the air, his pen twirling idly. Then he focused on her and frowned. The pen twirled again. "Are you worthy? Sexy blonde who savors a great cabernet wants to wile away hours with a man. Life is hectic enough. I need someone who appreciates a classic movie and a lazy Saturday night. Dave Eggers fans need not apply."

It *was* good. And he really thought she was sexy? Not that it mattered, of course. All she wanted was great dates with someone other than him.

And so it came to pass. Beth smiled and held out her hand. "Mr. James, I believe we have a deal."

2

Sexy blonde is looking for Mr. Right Now. Could that possibly be you? Need someone who knows how to laugh and is smart enough to make me smile.

HIS APARTMENT WAS CURSED.

For over an hour he'd been trying to work, but his concentration had been shot to hell. The constant buzzing of his cleaning woman's vacuum was driving him batty.

"Sophie!"

Still the buzzing continued. How the hell was he supposed to work in a war zone?

"Sophie!"

God bless it, the buzzing ceased.

Sophie appeared in the doorway to his study, clad in her latest red spandex jogging shorts, which accentuated curves she didn't need to advertise. Sophie, however, was a woman who'd never recovered from the eighties. "You rang, Mr. James?" she asked in the clipped English accent she used when she was feeling unservile.

"Can you please keep it down to a moderate level? Ten decibels? I'm trying to work here."

"That's interesting, Mr. James, because you're paying me to clean, and well, here I am, whoosh, whoosh, whoosh, cleaning my little heart out. Now you want me to be quiet. If you're determined to work, I can go into the living room and sit and wait. I'll just turn the TV down really, really low."

"You wouldn't mind?" Spencer asked. Usually Sophie wasn't the most cooperative of cleaning ladies. That's why she was cheap.

"Not if I'm still on the clock. And, Mr. James, I'm still on the clock."

Now why had he thought she'd suddenly become human? Someday he was going to hire a real cleaning service. Anonymous little elves who would clean and then disappear into the immaculately dusted woodwork. Someday.

"Vacuum," he snapped. "Vacuum until your little toes are sucked right off."

"Mr. James, are you flirting with me?"

Spencer shot out of his chair and growled. She grinned back at him and he slammed the door in her face.

AT SEVEN O'CLOCK, his stomach rumbled and he realized he'd missed lunch—and dinner. All afternoon he'd been listening to the interview tape, pretending to take notes, but so far the page was blank.

When she spoke, you actually could hear her smile in her voice.

Spence rubbed his eyes. Next thing, he'd be buying her flowers, and then maybe taking her on a date, and before you knew it, they'd be headed to divorce court and he'd be forced to endure fifteen more years of Sophie's slipshod work.

Hell would freeze first. Besides, Mr. Right Now was somewhere out there, just waiting for her, waiting to be graced with that careless smile, waiting to taste her strawberry kisses.

Well, Mr. Right Now could have her.

Not willing to go further down that strawberry-laden path, Spencer pushed himself back from his desk and walked over to the refrigerator. Now to play the new and exciting what's-for-dinner game.

Leftover pasta from Thursday night at Via Concetta. No. Leftover chicken from Wednesday night at Via Concetta. No. Would his luck change in the freezer? Frozen pizza. Frozen lasagna.

The lasagna wins, the crowd goes wild.

He popped the package into the oven, set the temperature and then slammed the door just as the doorbell rang. Odd. He hadn't buzzed anyone up. "You're going to have to wait. Don't embarrass me now," he said to his stomach.

Spencer didn't get many visitors. He tried to discourage the practice of stopping by without calling first. It tended to disrupt his concentration, and he'd forgotten how to make small talk, not that he really cared.

The bell rang again. It was most likely another salesman who couldn't read the No Soliciting sign. He should use a bigger font. Prepared to deliver his standard I'm-just-the-house-sitter line, he opened the door.

It was his onetime best friend, Harry, who mostly wrote sports for their paper.

"Spence, got three tickets to the Bulls game tomorrow. Want to come?" Harry said, shrugging out of his coat and slinging it over the chair.

"It's too early for April Fools, and too late for Halloween. Tell me you've just been drinking."

Harry collapsed on the couch and then stared up with that who...me? look he did so well. It was how he met all his women. "It was a genuine offer of hospitality."

"I've got plans for dinner already," said Spence, resigned to having company.

"Via Concetta?"

Spence flashed him a rude gesture often seen in the wilds of Los Angeles. "You can leave now."

Harry, who had never been to the wilds of Los Angeles, elected to stay. "I worry about you. This aloneness can't be good. The next thing you know, you'll be getting a cat."

Spencer shot out of his seat, the veins hammering away in his head, the pain only making him angrier.

"First off, since you are the primary reason that I'm suffering from all this aloneness, your concern smacks of hypocrisy. And I'm not getting a cat. Not even a dog. Not even a hamster. The little beasts are nothing more than glorified rats."

Harry shook his head in a mournful manner. "You're never going to meet another woman with that sort of attitude. You need to get back in the saddle."

"I can get back into the saddle anytime I want. You tell Joan that. In fact, I've got a date tonight," snarled Spencer, mainly to salvage what was left of his ego.

Never one to practice the fine art of subtlety—damn sports writer—Harry began to laugh. "A date? Returning a favor?"

"No."

"Mother's dentist's niece?"

"No," Spencer snapped.

"Some friend of Joan's that I haven't met yet?"

"Since you've been sleeping with her longer than I was married to her, that's highly unlikely."

"I waited four months. It seemed acceptable. Does this still bother you?"

"No." Spencer sighed. "Why don't you marry her?" he asked. Then he could at least save the alimony. Fifteen hundred a month, which was galling, since Joan's father could buy Spencer several million times over. Unfortunately, Mr. Barclay didn't believe in passing along his wealth to his daughter until he was dead, so now it was Spencer who was footing the bill.

Harry picked up the latest *New York Times* and began to read. "I've tried. She says no. It breaks my heart that her desire for revenge is bigger than her love for me. But you inspire that in women, Spence."

The phone rang, sparing Spencer a reply. "I bet that's my date now." In one smooth move he picked up the phone and opened the door for Harry to exit. "James here."

"Spencer, it's Beth. Beth Von Meeter."

After listening to her voice all afternoon, he still found it sent a tingle to places he thought were long dead. He turned his back on Harry, intimating intimacy. "Yes, I was hoping you would call."

"I think you're on to something. I've gotten four responses so far. Oops, make that five. And they all sound amazing."

Did she actually doubt his skills? "Of course."

"You wanted me to check in with you after I set up my first date, right?"

"Yes, I'll need to see you as soon as possible. Can you excuse me for a moment?"

"Certainly."

Spencer turned and glared at Harry. "Out," he said, arm stretched toward the door. If his arm were long enough to make it to hell, he'd have pointed there, too.

Harry gestured to the phone, then made pornographic hand signs, but he did pick up his coat and make his way to the door. Spencer walked over and slammed it right after him.

Then he took a deep, calming breath. "I'm sorry, Beth. You were saying?"

"We're going to see a play at the Steppenwolf tomorrow."

"Oh. What time will you be done?"

"It's a date, Mr. James, not a business appointment."

"You're right. What was I thinking? I'll meet you at one a.m. There's a coffeehouse across the street."

"I'm not dumping my date, who might be the most fabulous man I've met in my entire life, in order to go through the third degree with you."

As if he were just some two-bit stringer from Pomona. Spencer slammed his hand on the counter, immediately bruising his palm. Stupid moves like this were the prime reason he was healthier staying away from the human race. "As the man responsible for you meeting the most fabulous man you've ever met in your life, I would think some gratitude would be in order."

"Gratitude is not the emotion of the day. Try again tomorrow. I'll meet you Sunday morning."

Defeat came and smacked him on the head. "I'll

meet you at nine. Where do you live? We can find someplace nearby."

"All right," she replied, and then gave him her address. It was an apartment two blocks from his. Cheap, but safe and serviceable. Sad that an award-winning journalist was placed in the same caste as a coffee shop barista. Damn Joan. Why couldn't she just marry Harry?

"What's your date's name?" Spence asked, mainly because even while he was condemning his wife to alimonial purgatory, he was lining up lemming-style to be pushed over the edge again.

"Donald. Donald Hughes."

She sounded thrilled, as if the love of her life was going to be standing behind door number one. She'd been married before. How could she be so goddamn excited about the idea of doing it again?

"Wonderful," was all he said before he hung up.

Inside of him, there was the usual burning he felt at the start of every good story. Today there was something else. A different kind of burn, deep inside him.

A severe case of lust could do that to a man.

THAT EVENING, Beth spent two hours wheeling and dealing on eBay, before sending an IM message to Cassandra. The temporary money pinch she was in was improving and the man shortage was definitely improving in spades. Hallelujah!

Beth says: "You there?"

Cassandra says: "Yes."

Beth says: "Are you alone?"

Cassandra says, while inhaling the soothing scent of lavender: "If I'm entertaining, I'm not going to be sitting at the computer."

Beth says defensively: "I thought I'd ask. It's Friday night. Why are you sans a date?"

Cassandra says casually, too casually: "I felt like being alone."

Beth says: "You heard, didn't you?"

Cassandra says, shrugging: "I haven't the slightest idea what you're talking about."

Beth says: "Benedict."

Cassandra says: "Eggs."

Beth says: "You know exactly what I mean."

Cassandra says: "Yes, I heard."

Beth says: "What are you going to do?"

Cassandra says: "There is no rope painful enough to hang him from, so that's out. There's no river wide enough to ensure that he'd drown—so that's out."

Beth says: "Still feeling hostility for the former boyfriend, huh?"

Cassandra says: "Of course."

Beth says, because she's an optimist *and* a romantic: "He's going to show up. You know he will."

Cassandra says: "I'll handle it when he does. Are you going to the Christmas gala?"

Beth says: "It's family stuff. I have to go. You?"

Cassandra says: "Much too boring."

Beth says: "Lots of cool guys. You should go. And now to transition to all about Beth: Got a date tomorrow, got a date tomorrow, got a date tomorrow."

Cassandra says: "Stop the presses. Who's the latest?"

Beth says: "Personal ad person."

Cassandra says, while holding up thumb and forefinger: "Loser."

Beth says: "Hey, I resemble that remark."

Cassandra says: "No, you don't. We've had this discussion before."

Beth says: "You're right. This is the new, improved, no longer directionally challenged me."

Cassandra says: "Knock 'em dead, tiger."

Beth says: "You betcha."

DONALD HUGHES WAS a nice guy. He had a decent job—civil engineer for the city—was attractive and funny. In short, he was the ideal man. Beth kept checking him out during the play, casting quick glances just to see if he truly existed, or if she was overcompensating on his behalf and he was truly a wuss. No, he seemed to be real. A couple of times he caught her peeking, and smiled. The last time, he actually reached over and held her hand. It was the most romantic thing that had happened to her in almost eight months.

The play was very nice, but slightly depressing in that genuine Tennessee Williams manner. Afterward, he took her to a restaurant where she actually ordered dessert and coffee.

"I loved your ad. As soon as I read it, I thought, that's the kind of woman I want to meet."

"Thank you," she said, trying to look confident and modest all at the same time.

He launched into a discussion of wines. Boring. Then he started in on politics. Boring. After the discussion on the current state of the education system, her cell phone rang.

Uh-oh. Technically, she should have turned it off. But what if she got an important call?

She looked at the caller ID, but it wasn't familiar. Not that it mattered, because the discussion was really going nowhere. She wrinkled her nose at Donald. "Just a minute. Let me get that."

"Beth, it's Spencer James."

She hung up.

He called back. However, she wasn't mad enough to not answer.

"Don't hang up. You need to look more entertaining. You just look bored."

"Where are you?" she asked, realizing that the hair on her neck was now standing on end.

"Second table to the left, just at the edge of the kitchen."

She looked. He lifted a discreet hand.

She hung up.

The phone rang. Donald looked at her with confusion. "Are you having problems?"

"No," she said, laughing in that you-really-don't-want-to-know manner.

"You could turn your phone off," said Donald, full of wisdom.

Beth debated. In fact, her finger wavered over the power button. But when she glanced at Spencer, he shot her that arrogant look he did so perfectly. The phone rang again. "Just a minute," she said sweetly to Donald. "What?" she snapped at Spencer.

"You look bored. Smile at him. You're never going to get a man panting after you if you look like you'd rather be filling out your 1040 form."

Beth smiled in an absolutely enchanting manner—at Donald. "Happy?" she said into the phone.

But he had hung up.

DONALD DROPPED HER OFF about an hour later. He wanted to see her again, and she said okay, mainly because she knew it would be stupid not to give him a chance.

He kissed her, two and half stars on the Von Meeter kissing meter, and then left her alone. A true gentleman.

That made her sigh, but immediately after kicking off her shoes, she picked up her cell phone and dialed.

"Don't you ever follow me again without telling me," she exclaimed, even before Spencer said hello.

"I wanted to see where he would take you, watch the interaction between the two of you, see if there were electrical currents."

"Of course there were currents. A gazillion megawatts of currents. And if you hadn't been there spying over my shoulder, there would have been even more. Enough to light up Lake Michigan."

"Hmm. I didn't get that impression. Let me write that down. 'Currents. Gazillion megawatts of currents. Lake Michigan.'"

Beth never liked to be mocked, but she was capable of fighting dirty, too. She began taking off her skirt. "Look, Mr. James, I'm aware that you're used to doing things your way, but this is my life. I'm not going to be part of your own personal reality TV series."

Neatly she hung up her skirt on the hanger.

"I'm a journalist."

"I don't care if you're Superjournalist—" he swore at that "—you have to ask my permission."

"All right. Tonight was more of a trial run, anyway. When do you want to do the interview? Is now good?"

Beth pulled off her blouse and hung it up right next to her skirt. "No. I'm getting ready for bed."

"Well, throw on a robe. You had a cup of coffee. You're not going to sleep for another two hours."

"Wait a minute," she said, putting down the cell phone.

A wicked impulse had her bypassing the standard issue, worn-out sleep shirt and heading straight for the good stuff. She began rifling through her lingerie drawer, looking for her sexiest sleepwear. Slowly she pulled on the transparent peignoir, brushed her hair until it shone, then put on the necessary skin-care regimen. She stared in the mirror, pleased with the siren that appeared.

Finally, she retrieved the phone. "Spencer, you wanted to come over now?" she asked, making her voice low and husky.

He coughed. "It's best to strike while the information is right there at the top of your head."

She played with the silk ribbons, even daring to touch herself through the thin material. "I'll see you in the morning. Nine a.m., just like we planned," she said, still smiling.

"If that's what you want." She heard her own regret echoed in his voice.

Metaphorically speaking, he was the biggest slab of dark chocolate ganache she'd ever seen, a total caloric nightmare. She'd polish him off and be left with nothing more than fat thighs and an empty plate.

Tempting, but no.

After he hung up, she turned on the television in her bedroom and collapsed onto her bed. It wasn't until two hours later, when Cary Grant kissed Ginger Rogers, that she finally fell asleep.

HE WAS THERE EARLY the next morning. Not surprising, since he'd never really got to bed. After discovering work was useless, and then tossing and turning, trying to sleep, he'd finally taken matters into his own hands and dispensed with the aftereffects she had left him with. Then he'd managed to sleep, for a full three hours.

Joy.

The morning was cold and the sidewalks were damp with post-Thanksgiving slush. If he wasn't really excited about his article, he wouldn't be trudging through the mess at 9:00 a.m. Or so he told himself.

Eventually she showed up at the coffee shop, looking fresh and well-rested and with that damn smile on her face. Why was she always smiling? What the hell did she have that made her so happy all the time?

He stood when she came over and joined him.

"Good morning," she said, as if birds were perched on her shoulder, waiting to burst into song.

"If you're into those sorts of things," he said, surlier than usual.

"Are those circles under your eyes? Did you get up on the wrong side of the bed?"

Spencer, whose sense of humor was absent on most days, had almost no patience for her games right now. "Are you trying to tease me just to see how far I'll go? Do I look like the neighborhood mongrel who you're going to poke at with a stick until he bites back? You've never been bitten, have you?"

The smile cooled a few degrees. "No."

"Then I suggest you take your stick and put it away."

Her eyes cooled, as well. It could have been guilt he was experiencing, or so he told himself.

"That little lapse is best forgotten—pardon the breach. So where do we start now? You want to know about the date?" she asked, then proceeded to tell him every detail about the previous evening. He took notes, paying close attention to the exact moment when the smile crept back onto her face.

"When's your next date?" he asked, hating date number one with an unexpected passion.

"Tuesday evening. The Morton Arboretum is having a talk on flowers that bloom in the winter."

"Sounds very educational," he replied, thinking a root canal would be more fun. Chicago men seemed to be lacking in panache and creativity. If *he* were taking her out...

Damn.

He packed away his notebook and pen and took care of the check. "Great work. I'll see you on, when, Wednesday morning or Wednesday afternoon?"

"I've got to open up Wednesday morning, at 6:00 a.m."

"What about Wednesday evening?"

She winced. "Can't. Have a date. What about Tuesday night?"

He raised a brow. "I thought the post-date post-mortem was off-limits?"

"Since it's my schedule that's causing the problem, I'll make an exception. Where do you want to meet?"

"There's a restaurant a few blocks from here."

"You know, why don't you just come over to my place? That way we don't waste time with the commute, and I do have to be up early the next morning."

The words were innocent enough, and her eyes showed no sign of ulterior motives, but he was fast learning that she was a much better actress than anyone could guess.

Little Bo Peep did nothing without an ulterior motive. Maybe it was another one of her little poke-the-dog games. Maybe he didn't care.

The room got very quiet and an electric current

began to crackle in the air. A gazillion megawatts. Enough to light up the shoreline of Chicago—and Detroit, too.

Spencer stood, and if she noticed the electric charge that was currently tenting his pants, well, good for her.

She picked up her purse and followed him out. "I'll see you Tuesday night."

He met her eyes, but chose to remain silent. A man lived by his words, but he could die by them, as well.

3

Have you got what it takes? Sexy blond female wants to meet a man, and not just any man will do....

THE FLOWER TALK WAS cancelled due to inclement weather, so instead Beth and date number two, Michael Becket, ended up walking in the snow and looking at all the storefront windows that were decked out in their holiday finery.

Michael was a wonderful conversationalist, prone to burst out into bits of Broadway songs whenever he felt like it. At first she was embarrassed, but then she was charmed. He was nice. Everyone, including her parents, would approve.

The snow began to fall in earnest and he planted a kiss on her nose.

"You had a flake there," he said, by way of explanation.

Then his dark eyes got serious and dropped lower. "Uh-oh, I see another one." And then he kissed her mouth. It was a thorough kiss, presented with a skill that a woman should admire.

He certainly must kiss a lot—the kiss was a definite four stars on the Von Meeter meter. Yet he did nothing for her. Instead of being an active partici- pant, she was the aloof observer. Her pulse didn't speed up, her heart didn't skip one beat, and that was a damn shame.

When he pulled back, he gave her a soft smile, which should have sent her heart reeling.

Unfortunately, it didn't.

MICHAEL ACTED AS IF HE expected an invitation to stay, but Beth didn't feel up to company. And Spen- cer would be there soon, anyway. That was a situa- tion she didn't want to explain.

After Michael left, she fixed herself a cup of hot chocolate, adding two extra marshmallows—one point—as an added self-pity bonus, and that was when she saw the answering-machine light.

A message. Spencer was calling the whole thing off.

If she were a smarter woman, she would have felt relief rather than regret, because she knew he was strictly hands-off.

She pushed the button.

Beep. "Bethany, this is your grandmother. I have a little present for you that we need to discuss. Call me tomorrow. Ta-ta."

Beth smiled at the familiar voice. Her grand- mother was always thinking up new schemes to get

Beth involved in the family interests, but that wasn't Beth's road.

She wanted to go her own way, forge her own path. So far, it wasn't a big road, but Beth had always been content with that. She would call her grandmother and politely opt out of whatever was expected.

Then her buzzer rang and she realized Spencer was here.

Showtime.

Silently she repeated her hands-off mantra, but as she passed her reflection in the mirror, there was a smile on her face. It didn't scream *Hands off!* It was whispering *Hands on.*

SHE TOOK HIS COAT and hung it in the closet, noticing the bits of snow that were still mixed in his hair. It was such a casual look for a man who you'd never think would have a hair out of place. Her hand itched to brush it away, but that was too familiar a move.

"Need something to drink? Tea, coffee, hot chocolate?"

"I don't suppose you have any scotch?"

She entered the kitchen, sensing he was following her, and pulled a bottle from behind the marshmallows. No one could ever say she wasn't a perfect hostess. "Of course. Michel Couvreur."

"You drink that?" he asked, with the beginnings

of a smile on his face. She should have guessed it would take twelve-year-old scotch to make him smile.

"When the occasion calls for it," she answered, pulling out the appropriate old-fashioned bar glass.

He leaned a hip against the counter, reminding her exactly how small her kitchen really was. "What occasion calls for it?"

"When it rains," she said, watching the dark gold liquid splash into the glass. There was nothing as lonely as rain.

He took a sip and then wandered out of the kitchen, making himself comfortable on the couch.

"So, you want to know about Michael?" she asked, courting trouble by sitting next to him. But not *that* close.

He pulled out his notebook and pen. "Go ahead."

So she told him about the date. He laughed when she talked about the storefront windows, and not in a good way. When she mentioned Michael's talent for singing, he rolled his eyes. "It's pathetic what men will do to get women into bed."

"Did you ever think he might just like to sing?"

"No."

"So, Spencer James, why don't you give me a peek into the male psyche? Why couldn't a man just like to sing?"

"Men are programmed to want sex. It's very simple. When around a woman like yourself, every movement, every word, every note is a calculated ploy to further their own immortality by implanting themselves inside you."

Is that all this is? she wanted to ask. A ploy? A big drama to further his own immortality? She held her tongue, because the look in his eyes was sharp and intent, and it scared her.

"Are you going to see him again?" he asked, the pen tapping against the coffee table.

Beth nodded. "Sure. He's nice, a regular gentleman."

"A gentleman who sings," he said mockingly.

He did that so well—made fun of everything that might possibly be sincere. She twisted the green fringe on the edges of her throw. "According to you, that means he wants me. I should be flattered."

The pen flew off the table, and he swore when it rolled beneath the couch.

"I'll get it," she said, but it was just beyond her reach. She threw the afghan aside and slid off the couch onto the floor at the same that he did.

There they were, a whisper apart. She could see the pulse beating in his throat, smell the tangy soap that he used on his skin. Suddenly her mind was bombarded with the bits and pieces that made up Spencer James. At that moment, he ceased being a remote challenge and instead became something much more elemental.

She held her breath, waiting to see what he would do.

His gaze rested on her mouth, but he didn't touch her. Instead he reached under the couch, groping for his pen.

As he pulled it back out, his hand brushed against her breast. It wasn't quite an innocent mistake, because she was lying too close to him and they both knew it. Instantly her nipples peaked and she drew in a quick breath.

The next time, his fingers were slower, more precise, his thumb flicking against her breast as the edge of the pen stroked against the topside of her soft flesh.

The pressure between her thighs fired quick and hot, and she clenched her muscles to prolong the pleasure.

His eyes flickered, his golden lashes masking the need she had glimpsed.

Before she could react, it was over. The bit of accidental intimacy disappeared before it even started.

He climbed up onto the couch and took a long drag of scotch, then placed the pen on the table in a very exact manner. The message was clear. Not going to drop that pen again.

It wasn't the message she wanted. She wanted to sleep with him, wanted to see those cold eyes burn right into her. Normally she stayed away from men without that marriageable look in their eyes, but not him. Hands-off was no longer an option. Surely, if meaningless affairs worked for Cassandra, they could work for Beth, too.

Oh, God.

Beth shot him a nervous smile and adjusted her shirt, longing to borrow a sip of his drink to calm her nerves. However, her training in social situations kicked into play, and she cleared her throat. "Well, what else do you need to know?"

It was as if they were strangers. His voice was more clinical than usual, his eyes remote, never meeting her gaze.

Less than ten minutes later she was retrieving his coat and handing it to him. In one quick move, he pulled it on, and his hand was on the doorknob, pulling the door toward him.

"When's your next date?" he asked.

"I've got another one on Friday with Michael."

Spencer paused, a brief frown on his face, but then he recovered. Too telling. "How about I meet you Saturday morning? We could have a cup of coffee."

It was the frown that gave her courage, that split second of temper she read in his face. What caused a man without emotion to become angry? She knew it would be hands-on eventually. "I've got to work on Saturday morning. Opening again. Why don't you just come over on Friday night after I'm home? We're going dancing, so I'd be back by midnight."

The silence was deafening. *Big faux pas, Beth.* However, she noticed that he didn't drop his things and run.

"You're sure?" he asked, his eyes dark and questioning.

It was only a bit of a lie. She didn't work until noon on Saturday, but he would never know, and she liked the confined intimacy of him being here, of knowing that if she dared she could just reach out and touch him.

She smiled and nodded, her head buzzing from the hot chocolate. She told herself it was a sugar rush, but that was another lie.

THE OFFICE WAS BUSY on Friday, and Spencer was cursed with having to do his time in the Tempo section rather than his usual beat on the city desk. He had taken over the cubicle of an associate staffer out on maternity leave and used her computer to enter his latest story. "The Best of Chicago Dining" stared back at him from the screen. Yawn. Only a few more weeks until he'd be back where he belonged.

Harry came up and peered over his shoulder. "Savoir Faire. I've heard of that place. Can't afford it, but it looks pretty. Covered any fashion shows lately?"

"Coming to gloat?" said Spencer as he finished typing his article.

"No. I was thinking—"

"Dangerous."

"—I think we need to grab a beer, hoist a few. Guys' night out. Last night, I was covering the Bulls game and I came up dry. Completely ran out of red-blooded words. *Annihilated. Destroyed. Trampled. Shipwrecked.* I've written them all, but all I could think of was *beaten.* One measly 'beaten.'"

It was sad when a man lost his edge, became too complacent. Spencer had seen it happen to too many of his friends. His own father had been divorced five times before he died. After the second one, Spencer had learned it was only a matter of time. Men and women didn't operate on the same levels, and for some men, like Spencer, they never would. It was a lesson best learned early in life before they all bankrupted you.

Harry continued, "There used to be a time when I could ramble off forty-three synonyms for 'lost.' What's happening to me?"

"Marry Joan and you'll come up with eighty-seven synonyms for 'murder.' I've got a list. Why the itch to 'hoist a few'? She leaving you alone tonight?"

"She's flying to New York to shop," Harry replied glumly.

Spencer raised his eyebrows.

"Daddy's paying," answered Harry, which was a better answer than "Spencer's paying."

"I can't," Spence replied, his eyes fixed firmly on the computer screen in front of him.

"Come on," said Harry, in a tone that smacked of desperation.

"I have plans," he said.

"A date?"

"No."

Harry folded his hands across his chest and sat down on the corner of the desk. A bad sign, indicating immovability.

"I'm not going," repeated Spencer.

"Who is the mystery woman?"

"It's for work," said Spencer, because he clung to that belief very, very tightly. He didn't want to be involved with Beth, not with all her expectations. Flowers, gifts, giggling, and then a fourteen-carat noose that rested comfortably around the fourth finger of the left hand.

No, he was keeping his focus on the story.

Harry cocked a brow. "Sounds like a problem with your—"

"Dissect the Bears, not me."

"You sleeping with her?" asked Harry.

"No," said Spencer truthfully, although if the opportunity presented itself...

"Pity," said Harry, as he got up to leave. "You need a rebound, Spence."

A rebound? The Cubs would win the Pennant first. All he needed was a long night in the arms of one Bethany Von Meeter, and if he saw his chance, he'd take it.

4

SWF looking for a man who knows that hot chocolate is best accompanied by marshmallows, and that baths should last at least one hour, two if not alone....

BETH SAYS: "You there?"

Jessica says: "Yes. But I have a husband working on a proposal that will be done in approximately thirty-seven minutes. The clock is ticking... Go."

Beth says, her head hanging low: "I had a great date tonight."

Jessica says: "Great dates are good. Who was this great-date man?"

Beth says: "Michael."

Jessica says: "That's the second date for Michael, isn't it?"

Beth says: "Yes."

Jessica says: "It's 11:47 and you have a great date. Why are you online?"

Beth says: "*Had* a great date. He's gone."

Jessica says: "Sorry."

Beth says: "No, it was my idea that he leave."

Jessica says: "Okay, let's replay this scene. Great date, nice guy. Where did y'all go?"

Beth says: "Dancing."

Jessica says: "Great date, nice guy, dancing. You didn't ask him over, because"

Beth says: "I don't like him like *that*."

Jessica says: "Are you seeing him again?"

Beth says: "Next week."

Jessica comes out wielding a wet noodle and says: "If you do not like him like *that*, then you are wasting your time—and his. Find a man you do like like *that*."

Beth says: "He wanted to take me Christmas shopping. What woman could possibly turn down such a perfect male specimen?"

Jessica raises her hand and says: "I could."

Beth says: "He's everything I ever wanted."

Jessica says: "So do him."

Beth says: "But I'm not attracted to him sexually."

Jessica says: "Is he ugly?"

Beth says, defensively: "*No!* He's very handsome. Brown hair, brown eyes, great dimples, great bod. And he sings."

Jessica says: "Well, that would really get on my nerves."

Beth says: "I think it's sweet."

Jessica sighs and says: "You would. Do him. Then you'll know. If it's great—and he doesn't sing in bed—fabulous, problem is solved. If it's bad, he won't want to·see you again, anyway. Unless it's bad for you—or he sings in bed—and good for him, and then he'll want to do it again, and you'll be stuck because it's only good for him, and not you."

Beth says: "Thank you, Dr. Ruth."

Jessica says: "Just trying to help. Okay, seriously, if you don't like him that way, then move on to the next man. I mean, you've had twelve dates now. Surely there is somebody out there you do feel *that* way about."

Beth says: "No."

Beth says: "Yes."

Beth says: "No."

Jessica says: "I see."

Beth says: "I refuse to sleep with him. He's an ass—he's not very nice."

Jessica says, putting out her The Therapist Is In sign: "You are suffering from the interminable I-must-redeem-him syndrome. It is commonly found in caregiver type females. There is no cure."

Beth says: "I'm not going to sleep with him. I don't *like* him."

Jessica says: "Tsk, tsk, tsk. You are trying to reconcile your physical feelings with your emotional feelings and that is impossible."

Beth says: "So I sleep with him and I'm unhappy because I don't like him. Or I don't sleep with him, and I'm unhappy because I'm not sleeping with him. I'm doomed, aren't I?"

Jessica says: "Doomed is such a completely de-structive word. Let's just say you're destined for un-happiness."

Beth says: "I'm going to be strong."

Jessica holds up power fist and says: "Rock on."

Beth says: "Did you ever get like this about a guy?"

Jessica says: "Once."

Beth says: "So what did you do?"

Jessica says: "I married him."

Beth whaps her head on the keyboard and signs off.

SPENCER WAS EXACTLY seventeen minutes late. He wasn't about to show up early, and he couldn't make himself wait any longer than that.

He had brought two notepads and two extra Uni-ball pens because they were going to spend the next two hours working.

When she opened the door, she shot his poise and self-confidence straight to hell. In just one moment, the smooth, polished glass shattered.

He blamed it on the dress.

The image would be burned in his brain long af-ter his eyesight had faded. It was blue, a perfect blue. For a man who made a living by finding the exact word, he couldn't find any at all.

It clung to every part of her, the material soft and opaque, covering her as thoroughly and seductively as a rising mist. As he followed her blindly into her apartment, the soft lamplight cast shadows in that perfect blue that made his mouth go dry. There were curves in the shadows—soft, feminine curves that had his fingers reaching out to explore.

He locked his hands behind his back, Ulysses hearing the siren's call. His feet no longer obeyed his orders, instead racing after her like a foolish man who didn't realize he was about to be cast upon the rocks.

Then she turned and held out her hands, her blue eyes full of confidence. Was she actually going to touch him? His body tensed, every nerve laid bare by the mere promise of a caress.

"Your coat?" she asked, and disappointment shot through his heart. After he handed it to her, she brushed away the snow, her fingers gentle and soothing on the rough wool.

"Let's get down to work. I need to leave," he snapped, because he hated being vulnerable.

As he stalked into the living room, he spotted them. A pile of flowers spread out on the coffee table, in careless dishabille.

Daisies.

They were a cheap blossom, cheerful and simplistic. Exactly the flower for her, and he would never have thought about it at all.

"Do you need something to drink?" she asked,

playing the proficient hostess and attacking his courage all in one neat package.

"Please," he answered, kicking his pride into the dirt. His body was too distracted, his mind unable to concentrate except for the raw images of her— with him. He needed something to numb his sharp senses. Dull the buzz that was currently coursing through him.

This was work, he told himself.

After she poured his drink, he waited to see where she'd sit. She curled up in the chair that was three feet away from him, smiling in delight as she kicked her shoes off. He sank onto the huge couch. Alone. A hulking leather creation designed to hold four people, not just one.

Spencer pulled out his notepad and pen and started to fire off the usual questions. It was more of an interrogation than an interview, his voice getting sharper as the details of her evening became more intimate.

"Are you a dancer?" he asked.

She lifted one fantastic shoulder. "I don't embarrass myself."

"And your date?"

"He didn't embarrass me, either," she answered, her lips curving softly.

Spencer wrote down "SOB" on the paper, underlining it for emphasis. "Is he what you thought he'd be? Do you think he was truthful when describing himself?''

She picked up a daisy and turned it in her hands, those magical fingers stroking the petal carefully. "He's perfect, but he didn't say that. In fact, his ad was pretty blah.'' She started to laugh. "I know, you should redo his ad, too.''

"Not bloody likely,'' Spencer muttered under his breath.

"What's that?''

"Nothing.'' He forced himself to smile.

He was getting an exclusive into the workings of the female mind, and all he wanted to do was stab Michael Becket in the chest.

The man sang, for God's sake.

The worst part was listening to her talk about kissing him. Her cheeks flushed, her eyes turned soft and her lips parted. As he wrote, his pen stabbed at the pad, until finally he ripped the flimsy paper.

She stopped talking and looked at him, as if asking, *What are you doing?*

"If everything was going so well, why isn't he here?'' Spence demanded. *And why am I?* he thought, but he didn't ask that aloud. He didn't dare.

"Because I had to meet you.''

His head jerked up to determine exactly what her definition of "meet" entailed. But Bo Peep was giving nothing away. Her eyes wore the peaceful cheerfulness they always did; her lips were curved in a satisfied smile. No, the only clue that Bo Peep might be a little nervous was the way her hands were methodically shredding the daisy to bits.

She loves me, she loves me not.

"Very polite of you, but you could have called and rescheduled," he pointed out, nearly biting his tongue after he spoke. What was happening to his professional, passionless, detached demeanor?

"I stand by my word," she said, in a professional, passionless and detached manner.

He took a long sip of scotch, welcoming the numbing warmth.

Obviously *she* was not experiencing the sacrificial bonfire of lust that was burning his insides to cinders. No, *she* was just keeping a promise.

"I don't want to interfere in your life," he said, because if he said it often enough, it might become true.

"Yes, you do," she said. "You'll interfere until my life matches your idea of a scintillating story."

She leaned forward until he could smell her perfume, smell the grocery store scent of the daisies. Her voice began to shake. "Because that's why you're here. Isn't it? The story?"

Uncertainty flitted in her eyes. The need. The bonfire burned hot. Aha.

If he'd been Michael Becket, or Harry, or any of a

million other men who played games with women in this city, he would have looked into her eyes and pulled her into his arms, telling her in soft, seductive detail exactly how madly he wanted to make love to her.

Sadly, Mr. Casanova spilled his whiskey.

On purpose no less.

Instantly she was on her knees, wiping up the alcohol from the wooden table, the daisies falling to the floor.

He swooped down, and didn't look softly into her eyes.

He grabbed her chin in his hand and let her see exactly what he wanted from her. A smarter woman would have flinched.

Beth licked her lips.

Spencer James at his best wasn't nice. When experiencing the throes of lust, he was a man possessed.

He yanked her against him and his mouth ripped into hers, showing her quite explicitly how madly he wanted to make love to her.

He was muttering against her lips, raw and desperate, caught up in the damnable passion that was the worst sort of carcinogen.

She was just as wild. Her teeth nipped at his throat, her hands pulled his hair.

Some time in the next few hours she would be running back to that goddamn singing cowboy, but right now she belonged to Spence and he wasn't about to let her walk.

His mouth fed on her. Every inch needed to be possessed.

By him.

He rolled her over, his head knocking against a table leg, and quite happily he shoved the piece of furniture away.

At that moment, he could have shot to the moon with all the compressed power inside him. He had to have her, find the secret key that unlocked the pleasure within her. Tonight he'd discover it all.

He fisted his hand in her hair, staring into those blue, blue eyes, but he didn't see pleasure, only questions there. Questions he wasn't about to answer.

Instead, he pulled away the soft material that covered her breast, then pushed aside the demure lace of her bra. His fingers brushed at the silken perfection and felt the charge pulse through him. Pure lust.

His mouth took over where his fingers had been, first soothing the pink flesh, then sucking more insistently. Still, he needed more. His hands moved beneath her skirt, flicking the material aside, finding the bit of lace that covered her. It was a mere triangle tied to a string, a garment designed for seduction, not practicality, and he wondered whom she had worn it for. Her date? His hands twisted the tiny string and ripped it in two.

He didn't wait, but thrust his fingers inside her. Her body bucked and he watched her as she sighed with pleasure. Still her eyes were cognizant, and he wasn't content. His palm pressed against her bone, his thumb finding her nub, flicking hard, then softly, until her focus began to blur. Her lashes drifted low over her cheeks and the questions were gone.

Now it was time. He didn't want her thinking. His fingers began to work faster, her hips arching against his hand, meeting him stroke for stroke. Her head thrashed from side to side as she fought against her climax.

"Oh, no, baby," he said, pressing harder and harder.

There was no denying, nor fighting, the sexual heat that existed between them, and as long as he labeled it as such, he was safe.

They fought, two combatants determined to outlast each other, but she didn't have a chance. Her hands fisted in his shirt, twisting, knotting, but he wasn't about to stop.

Finally, her back arched, her eyes blind with pleasure, and at that moment he sent her over the edge, smiling when she screamed. This was where he needed her. Unthinking, raw, reduced to that most basic level, where his feelings for her resided.

Quickly he unzipped his fly, covered himself and then he was inside her. He wanted to be rough and unfeeling, but he couldn't. There she was, lying beneath him, exposed and damp. Trusting him.

Her eyes opened, clear and blue, seeing straight through him, and desperately he clung to his precepts. He thrust once, but still she watched him. Her lips parted, soft and inviting, and he couldn't resist. He lowered his head, gently kissing her. She didn't let him go, her fingers clasping his face, a magic caress against his cheeks. Her tongue slipped inside his mouth and slowly began to move, following the rhythm of their bodies.

He allowed her the moment, and began to follow the pleasure wherever it led. Just a momentary fling, a quick stress reliever to work out his frustrations. He rolled her over again, until she was lying on top of him, because he wanted to watch her, wanted to make sure her eyes stayed blurred.

And he told himself that, over and over, as he lost himself inside her.

BETH ROSE UP OVER HIM, watching the battle rage in his face. He was like quicksilver in her hands. For a split second the tender lover was there, and then, in a flash of heat, he had disappeared.

Not that it worried her. Beth had learned long ago that confrontations could take different forms and winning didn't necessarily mean that the conqueror knew he or she had lost. So she pulled the dress over her head, throwing it aside. This was her time, this was her victory.

She rode him easily, until his hands reached for the bra that was still dangling from her shoulders. She leaned back, putting her breasts just out of his reach, and then got rid of the pesky thing altogether. His gray eyes darkened to black and his breathing turned shallow. Very good.

Next she did something she'd only seen in the movies, something she'd only read about and never dared to try in front of a man. She touched her breasts, gently at first, hesitantly. It was her first try at sexual honesty, and he seemed to like it.

His hands grasped her buttocks, and his thrusts became more insistent.

Honesty made her bold. Her palms covered her breasts, sliding up and down her skin. He reached out to touch her, but she leaned back.

"Nuh-uh-uh," she said, taunting him.

Her fingertips walked down her body, to the place where they were joined, and a visible pulse pounded at his throat. Slowly she moved her fingers to where she could touch them both. She found the damp steel of his cock, and grasped firmly. There. His breathing stopped. His eyes flew open.

And she smiled.

He rolled her over on the rug, pulled out of her

and then flipped her onto her stomach. Obviously, smiling was the wrong thing to do.

She was just about to protest and then he was inside her again. Deeper he slid inside her, until she swore he was touching her heart. His body was hammering hers, a mating of two animals, rather than lovers. She could taste the rough threads of her carpet, smell the sharp kick of alcohol and hear his anguished breathing.

But she couldn't see him. She wanted to move, wanted to stare into his eyes, but he wouldn't let her.

Eventually her eyes drifted shut, and she let herself go, let herself ride the climax. Once, twice, and at the third edge of the wave, he stopped, his muscles tensing behind her. Then he collapsed on top of her, his weight heavy and his skin damp with sweat. His hands crept around her, exploring like a blind man. He touched her breasts, her belly, the nape of her neck.

Slowly, tenderly, his fingers soothed where they had stroked so angrily before. His lips murmured against her neck, words so low that she couldn't hear. Then he locked her tight against him, his hands joined over her heart, and they stayed that way for some time, until finally she was able to sleep.

WHEN BETH AWOKE, the room was bathed in darkness. He must have gotten up and turned off all the lights. She could hear his movements, and then he lifted her and moved her to the couch. At first she thought he was leaving, for she heard the rustle of clothes. But then he was next to her, his skin hot to the touch. His hand slipped between them and he felt her answering dampness, just before he slid inside her once more. This time he stayed by her side, face-to-face, though the darkness obliterated all sight. As he moved, her mouth explored his jaw, his neck, finally settling on his lips. Spencer stayed tense and unresponsive, but Beth wasn't about to give up. Finally he let go and joined her in the kiss.

Her heart cried with relief.

His movements were slow and sure, and she was pleased that he remembered what she liked. This time the climax came smoothly, gliding over her like water. And after he had found his own release, he locked her tightly against him, just as tightly as a child guarding a treasure.

For Beth, it was enough. She smiled against his shoulder, feeling his heart struggle against her own. It wasn't the smartest thing she'd ever done—the battle was going to be hell—but it really didn't matter.

Because now he'd done it.

Beth was in love.

HIS WATCH BEEPED at 5:00 a.m., just as it did every morning. She stirred once, but was a sound sleeper, content in sleep as she was in life. He cracked open her drapes, just enough to light the room with the first hint of morning. Down below, street crews were clearing the roads, salting away the pristine snow. Soon it would be dirty brown before disappearing altogether.

Emotions could be just as ephemeral. The heart was a cruel master and he wasn't about to get involved, be committed to someone, again.

Quickly he dressed, gathering his things. For a few jealous moments, he stood and watched her. She was so exquisite, her hair glinting gold in the faint light, her body open to his gaze.

He stuck his hands in his pockets, let his eyes touch her breasts, the curves of her hip and belly, the shadowy darkness between her thighs. Even her feet were perfect. Amazing. Not a single flaw to be found.

Her hands were tucked under her cheek as if she were dreaming of the love she was aching to find.

He wished her luck. Not that she needed it. It was only a matter of a date and a potent bottle of champagne and some poor sap would be falling all over himself to propose.

Slowly he ground his nails into his palms.

Then he noticed one of the remaining daisies from last night. Cheap things. He reached out and rescued it from the carpet.

Then he made his way to the door, making one short detour to drop the flower in the trash.

5

SWF needs perceptive man who will stop and smell the daisies right along with her....

THE NEXT DAY was agonizingly long. When she'd first started at Java4U, Beth had been happy just to have a steady paycheck. Now she thought she might be selling herself short. At the end of her first shift, after she'd made seventeen thousand lattes, her phone rang for the first time and she nearly knocked over her coworkers trying to reach it.

"Hello?" she said, her heart pumping wildly.

"Bethany, this is your grandmother."

Her heart calmed itself. "Yes, *Grand-mère?*"

"Come by the house this evening. We need to talk."

"I have to work a double shift today."

"Well, don't you get some type of a break? This is important and it won't take more than a few minutes."

"Yes, *Grand-mère,*" she said, before hanging up. Then she called her answering machine at home, just in case, but there were no new messages. Damn.

SPENCER SPENT THE ENTIRE Saturday doing chores in his apartment. He cleared out old magazines, repaired the leaky showerhead in the bathroom, even painted the radiator in his bedroom a cleaner shade of white, all the while listening to CNN at ear-blasting volume.

Anything to keep his mind off exactly how he'd screwed up his life last night.

Around dinnertime, Harry stopped by.

Spencer flung open the door and scowled. "Come in. Don't stay long."

Harry stepped inside, grinning. "Got another date?"

"No," said Spencer, appalled to hear regret in his voice.

"How's life in the Tempo section?"

"I know where the shoe sales are now, if that's what you're asking."

Harry laughed. "You're miserable, aren't you?"

"Did you only come here to gloat? It speaks volumes about your character."

"Did you want tickets to the *Nutcracker?* I can't go."

"Desperate to get out of it, aren't you? Don't try to pawn them off on me."

"Well, maybe Joan can get rid of them."

The buzzer sounded. It was a long, insistent blaring.

Spencer shot Harry a pained look. "You had to bring the entertainment, didn't you?"

"I told her to stay in the car," Harry explained, in an almost believable manner.

Spencer jammed the button to buzz her up, and soon he was greeting his ex-wife at the door. He took note of the new Louis Vuitton handbag she was carrying. Now that he was working in fashion—temporarily—he knew exactly how much those damn things cost. That was his holiday bonus she wore on her arm.

Harry grabbed her just as she was getting ready to sit down. "No need. Spencer won't take the tickets." Then he turned to Spencer. "Why don't you take your date?"

"Who's the latest victim?" Joan asked, settling herself in Spencer's favorite chair.

"You don't know her."

She swung her leg, and he eyed the shoes she was wearing. Expensive, no doubt. "You're making it up, aren't you?" she said, obviously implying he *would* lie about something like that.

"Beth Von Meeter," Spencer spat.

"Von Meeter? Blond, perky, nice?"

Spencer stared. He'd never considered the possibility that his former wife might know Beth, but the Von Meeter family would run in the same circles as his ex. "That's her."

"Oh, Spencer. She's *all* wrong for you."

Harry raised his brows. "And I suppose you're the right type for him?"

Joan froze, studying Harry, long and considering. "God, no. But he'll chew her up and spit her out. Unless she's changed?" Joan asked, turning back to Spencer.

He shook his head. "No."

Joan smiled at Harry and patted his cheek. "Now, see? I told you I'm always right."

Spencer felt inclined to warn Harry, just in case he hadn't realized it yet. "She is, you know. Always."

Harry sighed. "I know."

Joan sank farther into the cushions and shook her head. "We should all go out together. A double date."

Spencer would rather spend his days writing obituaries. "No."

Joan laughed. "It was worth a try. Care for dinner this evening? I worry about you, Spence, you're losing weight."

In other circumstances, such concern might be touching. "Harry, can't you control her?"

Harry just looked smitten. "No."

"Okay, I can see I'm not welcome here. So, will we see you at the Von Meeter Foundation winter gala, then?" Joan asked, watching him as if she expected him to say yes.

"Why would I be there?" He hated charity functions. She knew that.

She studied her nails, scarlet-tipped talons that could carve up a man. "Well, considering your new girlfriend is the daughter of the hostess, I just assumed…"

It should have been an easy decision for him. Either blow off the whole thing, or create an elaborate ruse to bluff his way into a date, where he would be trussed up in a penguin-suit rental. With Beth.

That's where the allure was. It was an opportunity to steal into her litany of dates, but this would be his night. And it would all be under the guise of shmoozing and research dollars. No messy declarations. No explanations necessary at all.

"Oh, the foundation benefit—it slipped my mind. Of course I'll be there. You know how I hate the damn things."

"Yes, I do, so watching you suffer will make it all the more enjoyable."

"Harry, shut her up. Please."

Harry smiled and sat down on the arm of her chair. "Of course." And then Spencer watched as Harry kissed his ex-wife. Quite efficiently. Even more amazing, Joan was curling her arms around his neck, and suddenly Spencer was feeling like a third wheel in his own apartment.

"Joan, if you love him, marry him," Spencer pleaded.

She turned and smiled, like a cat who had sampled both the canary and the cream. "Not until I turn fifty. So you have another seventeen years of alimony."

Smart girl, she was out the door before he could deck her.

As soon as five o'clock hit and Beth got her dinner break, she took a cab over to her grandmother's estate in Lake Forest. It was the family house, a place she had loved when she was growing up. Though eventually she'd realized the gate that kept her inside kept the world out, as well.

That didn't stop Bath from wanting to visit, but she always felt a special thrill whenever she left. The gate closing behind her meant that she was free. Back outside, everything came alive.

After she was buzzed in at the gate, she wandered into the fairy-tale world of Chicago money decorated in snow. The house was an old gothic, with tall, narrow, diamond-paned windows. Miniature fir trees, decorated with lights and bows, perched merrily on the upstairs balcony and at either side of the grand entrance. Giant sprigs of greenery and red ribbons hung from the twin spires. The front door had a wreath attached, a wreath Beth had seen every Christmastime for almost thirty years, that still smelled of cinnamon and pine.

Her grandmother loved Christmas just as much as she did.

When Sandoval opened the door, Beth found herself grinning. She couldn't help it.

Sandoval was the doorman, the butler, the general who ran the household, and he greeted her warmly. "The empress is expecting you," he said, taking her coat, and showing very little disdain as he eyed the worn creation. It wasn't Brooks Brothers, but it was her lucky coat, and she'd bought it on her own, so that made it twice as nice.

As Beth entered the parlor, her grandmother rose, a tiny woman with eyes that missed nothing and cheekbones that were still the subject of the style section in the paper.

"*Grand-mère,*" Beth said, and swallowed the tiny woman up in a hug.

"Bethany. Let me look at you." She held her out for inspection, shaking her head sadly. "A good clothing allowance would do wonders for you."

Beth laughed. "On my salary?"

The blue eyes sharpened. "And that's just what we need to talk about. Sit down."

And here it came again. The talk. Family responsibilities. Image. Crap.

Beth smiled politely and sat, her legs automatically assuming the Von Meeter cross.

"Do you remember the teahouse that opened down on Printers Row?" asked her grandmother.

Beth shook her head. "No."

Her grandmother frowned. "Well, I bought it."

Whoa. Not quite the responsibility lecture she'd been expecting. Beth started to relax. "Cool. That's exactly what you need—a business to keep you active. And a tearoom is perfect."

Her grandmother poured a cuppa and sipped daintily. "Yes, I thought it would be nice, but I need a manager. Someone I trust. Someone for whom only par excellence will be accepted, and who has the drive to implement it, as well."

Ah, the plot thickens. Beth coughed. "I'm sure there are any number of able-bodied professionals that can achieve your vision."

"I want you."

And yes, there it was. Family Responsibility. Capital *F*, Capital *R*. "I have a job."

"Yes, my dear, you have a *job,* but no *career.* You need to think about doing something with your life."

"And why? Aren't there people out there who understand that the intrinsic purpose of life is to live?" It wasn't a compelling argument, but it was the best she could do on short notice. It wasn't as if she didn't *want* to do something with her life, but she wasn't really good at anything. Well, except that she made a mean cup of coffee, knew how to carry on idle conversation and could write lurid headlines.

"Yes, there are people like that, but you're not one of them."

"Yes, I am, *Grand-mère*," she answered softly.

"Your mother's too soft on you."

Beth's fingers dug into the arms of the crushed velvet chair. "Don't you dare pick on Mother. This is my life. I pick and choose roads." Actually, she didn't really choose roads, because if she did then everyone would know how limited her skill set actually was.

"Your roads are permanently under construction. I'm offering you the highway, dear."

"No." Beth rose, choosing to run. "And now if you'll excuse me, I have a real job to get back to."

It was a lie. A small one. She didn't have a real job; she had something that gave her a paycheck. Big whoop.

"Will you at least stop by? See the place? I think you'd be perfect."

"No. I know you. You'll get your little hooks into me. 'Oh, the chintz covers will be darling! And doilies, we must have more doilies.' And pretty soon the papers will be filled with talk of Muzzy Von Meeter's Midas touch, and I'll be relegated to a 'family member who works there on weekends.' I want a project of my own."

As she said the words, she realized they were true. She did want a project of her own. Preferably something with a high level of anonymity, though. Just in case it wasn't a rousing success.

"Like what?" asked her grandmother, perfectly arching one brow.

"I haven't found it yet."

"We'll talk later," the dowager murmured, knowing the wisdom of a temporary retreat. She pulled at the bell that hung next to the marble fireplace. "Sandoval, get her coat, please."

Beth walked into the entryway, completely ignoring the tall Christmas tree in the foyer. The mood was ruined.

"Think about it, my dear."

"Of course I will." I Was A Spoiled Heiress: Breaking Free and Going Broke. Beth smiled and held out her arms as Sandoval helped her into her coat. Instantly she realized the mistake. "This isn't mine."

Her grandmother held out a hand, her eyes firm. "Of course it is. Just consider it an early Christmas present. The winter's going to be so brutal and you'll need something to wear to the foundation benefit. You are coming, aren't you?"

There was the order, the command, the obligation. But it had been three years since she'd last been to the gala, and maybe obligation was weighing more heavily on her shoulders than usual. Beth smiled. "Probably." And then she took off the cashmere coat and handed it to Sandoval. "Give it to charity. Since the winter's going to be so hard."

JUST BEFORE CLOSING TIME, Mickey called. "We've been Christmas shopping and are in dire need of refreshments. What time are you done?"

"Thirty minutes," she said, counting the minutes, the seconds, the milliseconds. Oh, her feet were killing her.

"Smegging perfect. Meet us at Brick's when you're free. We'll be the ones in the corner buried beneath Macy's bags."

Beth pulled out the mop, holding her nose. She hated the mopping most of all. "That would be nice." It'd been one of those days, but soon it would be over. First, the offer from her grandmother, then the toaster at work had gone on the fritz and everyone wanted their bagels warm. To top it all off, Spencer *still* hadn't called.

Definitely a day she wanted to forget.

"I'll be there," she promised, figuring that if she was very disciplined next week, she could swing the four extra points for a double-shot martini.

BRICK'S WAS COVERED in Christmas lights and mistletoe and Beth got a thrill just walking in the door. Even her grandmother couldn't ruin this. Spencer couldn't ruin this. Not even mopping could ruin Christmas for her. It was a season when people were nicer, and everyone wore a smile for absolutely no reason in the world.

Just as Mickey had said, she found them in the

corner, with a pile of bags covering the table and the floor.

"Somebody is going to steal all that stuff."

Cassandra held out a dramatic hand. "They wouldn't dare. I've been taking kick-boxing lessons."

Beth sat down and swiped Mickey's drink, nearly spewing it out after she tasted it. "Tonic water?"

Jessica lowered her voice to a stage whisper. "She's not drinking. We've all decided they're trying to reproduce."

Mickey rolled her eyes. "That is *so* not true. Somebody doesn't drink and you just leap to all sorts of incorrect conclusions."

"There's nothing wrong with getting pregnant," Beth said, although the idea of small babies terrified her. All in all, she thought she'd make one terrific aunt.

"Unless you're not planning on getting pregnant, and people start looking at you funny because they think you're trying and just being unsuccessful," said Jessica.

A fire started in Mickey's eyes, so Beth opted to change the subject. "So, what did you buy Dominic for Christmas? You know, the present that you're planning on telling everyone you bought for him. And no, you can't hold out on the other, more secret and sexy one, either."

"I got him a book on plants and some other things."

Cassandra smiled. "It's sheer and black, and the man is going to need a bypass before she's through with him."

Beth laughed. "You picked it out, didn't you?"

Cassandra just smiled.

"Okay, enough of this crap. I want to hear about the dating game. What's the latest score?" Jessica asked.

Beth sighed. "Date number fourteen is a winner."

Mickey choked. "You went on fourteen dates? And you're still alive? Geez, do you have a fairy godmother, too?

"She had a professional fix up her ad," said Cassandra, and they all looked at Beth with respect. Beth preened. It sounded fabulously sophisticated.

"There're people that do that?" Mickey asked, still looking horrified.

"He's a journalist. He wanted to do an article, so we struck a deal."

Jessica held up her hand. "Wait a minute, there's going to be an article about your dating experiences? Who does he write for? This isn't some *Playboy* thing, is it?"

"No, he writes for the *Herald*."

Jessica's mouth fell open. "No kidding. You're going to be famous."

"No, he's not going to use my real name. I made

sure. My mother would have a total fit." Beth paused. "Oh, I hadn't really considered all the ramifications of that. Maybe I should reconsider?"

Mickey popped a chip in her mouth. "Nah, you're not the rebel type. Anonymity is good."

"So, how are things?" asked Jessica.

"They're good," said Beth, eyeing the chips covertly. Not worth the extra points. Spencer had cost her about two pounds and she wasn't going to gain any more.

Thoughts of Spencer were depressing, and she considered confessing that she'd just had wild monkey sex with a Scrooge of a man and then promptly fallen in love. It was the ultimate dysfunctional affliction, so she elected to keep quiet. "I'm doing good," she added.

"So who's the best candidate so far?"

And she spent the rest of the evening telling them about Michael. Every marvelous thing he'd said. And by the end of the night, they were all in agreement.

Michael Becket was absolutely perfect.

6

SWF who has been looking for love in all the wrong places needs a non-toadlike male to practice kissing.

HE DIDN'T CALL. She had a date with Michael on Sunday, the perfect Michael Becket, and Spencer didn't call her to meet afterward.

Beth hadn't thought there was anything that could ruin *Casablanca* on the big screen. However, now she realized that the Un-Call was capable of ruining anything.

It was a telling sign. The sex had been a momentary distraction, the intimacy of the evening combined with close quarters.

When she kissed Michael good-night, she even used her best arm-curling-around-the-neck move, just to get into the spirit of things. The spirit remained unmoved.

By Tuesday afternoon she had convinced herself that it didn't mean a thing and that she'd better talk herself into love with Michael B., who was, as they'd all decided, *perfect*.

Of course, at the exact moment when she decided that, Spencer called—as men do, just to freak you out.

"When can we meet?" he asked.

"I have to work on Thursday and I'm going shopping with Michael on Friday. I could pencil you in for forty-five minutes on Saturday morning." Two could play at cool sophisticate.

"How about Friday night? After your date?"

Oh, he was after sex again. Her pulse began to race, but she wasn't stupid. "Not this time," she said, letting him infer what he will. Preferably that she wasn't going to be alone on Friday night.

"Maybe you'll be busy on Saturday morning, as well," he muttered, and she wouldn't have been human if she didn't admit to being pleased. "Saturday lunch, then," he amended.

"I could do that," she said.

"I'll meet you at Bar Louie, Dearborn Station. Two o'clock."

Okay, public place. That was an easy one to read. Not going to be alone with her again. Which meant one of two things: one, no relationship here, or two, bad sex. She shook her head. No, the sex had been fabulous. It was the relationship thing. Major sticking point with him.

"Make it three. Café Toulouse," she said, just to be contrary.

CAFÉ TOULOUSE WAS excruciatingly well lit for a man with the lingering effects of a hangover. Spencer had spent Friday night pretending to work, but actually had spent most of it staring at a blank page and the bottom of a bottle of scotch.

It didn't help. He was still seriously contemplating the murder of one Michael Becket.

When she showed up—eight minutes late—he took in the cheery smile, the flushed cheeks, and wondered who had been sleeping in Bo Peep's bed last night.

"Good afternoon," she said, all perky-like.

"You're late."

"I know," she said, seating herself and offering zero explanations for being tardy.

The waiter appeared before Spencer could reply, which was probably a good thing considering his pisser of a mood.

After the server handed Beth the menu, she shook her head. "You know, I don't think I'm very hungry."

"We're in a restaurant," he replied.

She snapped the menu closed. "I guess I'm just being silly. Let's go for a walk instead."

Spence rose, helping her into her coat. "The restaurant was your idea."

"But it's such a lovely day."

"It's sixteen degrees, with a windchill factor of three."

"I love winter."

"You and the heating companies."

She took his arm and cuffed him lightly in the shoulder. "Oh come on, loosen up. What's your problem today?"

He noticed that she included the "today" qualifier, which meant she didn't think he was a bastard all the time. In his eyes, that was progress. "I don't have a problem."

They strolled in silence down the quiet street, passing the old Dearborn train station with its redbrick facade. Only a few foolish diehards were braving the elements today.

"I can't write when we're walking," he said, just to remind her that this was work.

"That's all right. There's all day to write."

"No, I have a deadline," he said flatly. "Which I can't meet when we're walking."

She sighed, and when she spied the covered bus stop, she steered him over and they sat down. "There. Now we're not walking."

So why did she have to make this so difficult? They weren't walking, but it was still nose-numbingly cold.

Although there was one good thing about the below-zero windchill. It kept his loins from springing to life. Even bundled up in his warmest winter coat, he could still remember smooth skin, silky hair brushing against his chest.

Damn it. His loins sprang to life.

The kid at the corner of the glass shelter eyed them nervously. Spencer smiled, effectively dismissing him.

"All right. So tell me about last night," he began, pulling out his notebook and pen.

She stuffed her hands in her pockets and wiggled for warmth. "It was perfect."

Perfect, he thought to himself. "I suppose he sang to you."

She missed the sarcasm. "No, he took me to the *Nutcracker*."

"How special."

"It really is. I used to go every year with my family...." Her voice trailed off.

"And he guessed that you'd love it," he finished for her. "Or did you tell him?"

"Oh, no, he guessed."

Of course. "So is it true love?"

She considered it—damn her, she considered her answer. Finally, she shook her head and he began to breathe. "No. But he's the sort of man that over time you can't help but fall in love with."

Unlike one Spencer James.

A bus pulled forward and the kid hopped on, leaving them alone. Spencer waited for the engine noise to abate before he asked his next question. "What would your family think of him? Would he meet the Von Meeter standard?" he said, struggling to find a flaw in her perfect man.

She looked at him, surprised. "You knew?"

He shrugged. "I'm a reporter. It's an unusual name. It's not hard to figure out."

Her chin stuck out, amazingly militant for such a little piece of Dresden. "They don't try and dictate what I do."

"Yeah, I can tell," he murmured.

"Well, that was rude," she snapped.

"You're too sensitive. It's the truth."

"The truth is often rude, but that doesn't mean you're supposed to say it."

"I'm a journalist. It's what I do."

"Can we stop talking about my family?"

"Oh, right. Tell me more about Michael."

And she went on. And on. And on. *And on*—in the way that only lovesick females can do. He learned every exacting detail about Michael. His favorite foods, the last great movie he saw and the cute story about his childhood puppy, Rufus.

Except Spencer still couldn't tell if she had slept with him. Michael, not Rufus.

"I bet he has a tattoo," he said, prying for information.

"Why does that matter?" she answered, not confirming nor denying.

"It's the height of stupidity to brand yourself with one image, or even worse, one name that will stick with you for the rest of your life."

"I think it's romantic," she said with a lengthy sigh.

He looked up, surprised. "Why, for God's sake? It's unhygienic, and the practice of marking up your body is barbaric."

"It's a sacrifice. I'm sure the concept is foreign to you—"

Spencer cut her off before she got carried away with the insults. "So, he does have a tattoo?"

"I don't know," she murmured. Then she looked up sharply. "And I don't think it's any of your readers' business to know it, either."

He scratched out the blank line on the paper. "All right. Forget the tattoo."

"Thank you," she said primly.

"You're still going out on other dates, aren't you? This isn't an exclusive situation, is it?" he said, still pretending to write.

"Of course it's not an exclusive situation. I'm not tying myself down to anyone..." she looked up from beneath her lashes and smiled "...yet."

"Now that you've been exposed to the vulnerabilities of the stronger sex, you're out for blood, aye?"

"It's not mercenary to date more than one man. I like to think of it as research."

Research? He shot her a look. Was that what the other night had been? Research? "You're going to write a tell-all?" he said, laughing nervously.

"You don't have anything to worry about," she said, patting his hand as if it were the head of an obedient puppy.

"I know that," he said, glossing right over any hint of a relationship. "When's the next date? Where are you going?"

"There's a lawyer from Skadden Arp who's taking me to an art exhibition."

"Thrilling."

She studied her gloves. "It'll be okay."

"So what about the Foundation benefit? Are you going to take Michael with you? Vet him for approval?"

"No. Bad idea."

"Why?"

"I like keeping some things private."

"And that is why you're putting your dating habits in a newspaper with a readership of five hundred thousand?"

"No, I'm doing that to get good dates. No, great dates."

"And have you?"

"Oh, yes. The absolute best."

"I need a favor," he asked, pressing his luck.

"No," she said, smiling politely.

"You don't need to be rude."

The smile widened to a grin, two watts brighter than the sun. "What can I do for you?"

Suddenly he had to force below-freezing air into

his overheated lungs. He lowered his head, exorcising the image of her mouth on him. "I want to go to the benefit."

"That can be arranged. I'll get you two tickets."

And she was going to make it difficult. "I'd like to take you."

She cocked her head and grew very quiet. "A date?"

Quickly he hastened to correct the mistake. "No. Business. For the paper."

"So why am I needed?"

He struggled to find an answer to that stubborn question. "For the paper," he repeated, unable to think of anything better.

"Ah, one of those for-the-good-of-the-nation dates? It seems that a journalist should be able to think of something better than that, if *business*—" she stressed the word heavily "—requires you to have a date. With me."

"I need to go. I'd like to spend the evening with you. That's all," he stated. She stared at him with those questioning eyes, and he pulled up the collar of his coat. His dating days, if they could ever be called that, were long over. He'd never gotten the courtship ritual correct, and wasn't patient enough to learn.

Finally she smiled. "In that case, I'd love to have you escort me to the benefit. There is one catch."

"Isn't there always?"

"You have to check the attitude at the door. I don't go on dates with jerks. It's bad for my image."

"I wouldn't embarrass you," he said.

The blue eyes turned on him, assessing, and as always, full of questions. "You'll live to regret it if you do."

"It's a date," he said, hoping that she didn't notice that it was sixteen degrees out and he was sweating.

IT JUST SO HAPPENED that Café Toulouse was three blocks from the tea shop her grandmother had just bought. Imagine that. Beth steered them down Polk Street and stopped when they reached the small entrance.

"You're looking for something to drink?" he asked. "They're not open for business yet."

"I know," she said, testing the old brass doorknob. Locked.

She moved close to the window, so close her breath fogged the glass, and stared.

"Why are we here?" he asked.

"It's my grandmother's place."

"Ah. You've never seen it before?"

"No."

"There's a man inside. I bet if you smile prettily and introduce yourself, he'll let you look around. And I bet it's not sixteen degrees inside, either."

"You are such a difficult man."

"I know," Spence said with a smile.

Just to prove her wrong, he knocked on the door, pounded, and then bellowed in the keyhole until the older gentleman opened it.

Beth smiled prettily. "Hello, I'm Beth Von Meeter. Muzzy's granddaughter."

Instantly the gentleman transformed. "Come in. I'm Jonathan Abercrombie, her new business manager. She mentioned that you would be managing the café."

Spencer turned and watched her, his gray eyes measuring her abilities. "Managing the café?"

Beth kept the smile fixed to her face. "No. That's *Grand-mère*, always leaping to conclusions."

"Why don't you look around? We've started some of the renovations already. Your grandmother is a very particular woman."

"Yes, I know. It runs in the family."

Then she began to look around. Really look. Seeing what lay beneath the dust and the barren walls.

"We're going to have some Persian rugs covering the floor by the bar. Hardwood everywhere else."

"Polished oak," said Beth.

"Don't you think tile would be more practical?" asked Spencer.

She merely stared, hating the idea of the loud echoes tile would cause.

"Polished oak sounds marvelous," he said, as he walked across the creaking floor.

Mr. Abercrombie trailed after them. "She wanted flocked velvet wallpaper," he interjected.

"With a chair rail, of course," Beth said, running her fingertips over the plaster wall. It would take lots of work.

"Of course," said Mr. Abercrombie, now taking notes.

Spencer shook his head. "Stains. The stains will kill you. And God help you if you end up with high humidity. Mold."

"Will you please stop trying to help?"

"Ah, but you're not running the place, so it shouldn't matter." He smiled slowly. "Should it?"

Beth elected not to respond, and instead concentrated on the back room. "The kitchen will be here?"

"Yes. We'll have desserts and finger sandwiches. Nothing heavy."

"Perfect, but the tea bar needs to be out front. A gleaming silver samovar that's as high as the ceiling. And waiters. Young, handsome, model types in black ties and coats."

Spencer folded his arms across his chest, leaning against the wall. "That's a whole lot of input from someone who isn't interested," he said.

"Maybe I am interested," she answered, disliking the amusement in his eyes.

"I don't think you're up to it. Imagine the work, the commitment. And a tearoom? Outdated and useless."

"Your confidence is hitting me right here," she said, beating a fist against her chest.

He shrugged. "I just call 'em like I see 'em."

"I know, I know...you're a journalist."

"So, are you going to give it a shot?"

"No."

"Didn't think so," he said.

"And why not?"

He sent her a knowing look. "Well, it's a long way from Java4U."

It *was* a long way from Java4U. It was stately and elegant—with really filthy windows. But the windows could be cleaned. "I could do it if I wanted to."

"Maybe."

Beth backed up against the dust-covered wall and then slid down to the floor. Through the convenient curtain of her hair, she looked up at him, trying to read his thoughts. Could she really do this? It sounded challenging, frightening—thrilling.

Just like everything in her life right now.

Spencer sat down beside her. "It really could be a great place," he said softly. "Although I'm not sure about the waiters. Too stuffy."

"The old ladies will love it," she answered, sure of herself. If there was one thing she knew, it was females.

He shrugged, looking very innocently befuddled. "I hope you know what you're doing."

Inside she trembled, because she was scared to death, but she was fast learning to put up a good front. So she shook back her hair and looked him square in the eye. "Of course I do."

7

SWF with newly acquired independent streak is seeking SWM. Need someone who is nurturing and sensitive and encouraging. Bonus points if you're good-looking.

THE GALLERY OPENING WAS a true yawner, and after a few frantic cell phone calls made from the bathroom, Beth conned Cassandra into showing up, as well.

Larry the Lawyer was one of those "nice types" who tried so hard to be nice he ended up grating on your nerves. He had blond hair, not the tarnished gold of Spencer, but a California blond. Nice. His eyes were gray-green, in a cologne-model sort of manner. Another nice. Still, they didn't snap like Spencer's, or heat up when she smiled at him.

As Beth wandered the hallway hand in hand with the very nice Larry the Lawyer, she examined the modern sculptures, all the while thinking of Spencer. He had a way of occupying her thoughts, and she wondered if she occupied his thoughts, as well.

About that time, Cassandra showed, dressed fabulously, of course. Marvelous black silk trousers, black sheer blouse and a long white coat.

Beth performed the introductions to Larry the Lawyer and watched in amusement as he succumbed to the first throes of Cassandra lust.

"So you're a lawyer?" asked Cassandra, starting with the small stuff.

Larry must have assumed she was flirting with him, because his voice dropped one octave. "I work in the district attorney's office. You like lawyers?" he asked.

Beth almost warned him that Cassandra had no other mode when dealing with men, but decided it was more fun to just watch.

"Only the dead ones," Cassandra said, giving him a sugary wink.

Larry looked confused, but he seemed one of those never-say-die sort of men. He looked at Beth. "You know, I need a date to my company Christmas party next week. Why don't you go with me?"

Beth smiled politely. *Not in your wildest dreams, Larry the Lawyer.* "I'm sorry. I've already made plans." Immediately Larry turned to Cassandra, as if asking Beth had been merely a courtesy.

"Well, maybe you're free? What do you say? Drinks, dancing, breakfast?" he asked, sotto voce.

Oh, now he'd done it. Beth began to smile. Nothing like a little fireworks, and Cassandra didn't disappoint. She linked her arm through Beth's. "I don't do men."

Beth smiled and shrugged, willing to play happy ambisexual in order to erase Larry from her life.

However, Mr. Never-Say-Die wasn't about to roll over yet. "Really? You two? Have you ever... With a guy... It'd be pretty fun."

Beth decided not to respond to that. Instead she led Cassandra away and they took a cab back to Brick's. Date Number Fifteen was definitely a No.

THE BAR WAS NEARLY EMPTY for a Tuesday night.

"I think you should go to the gala. Seriously," said Beth. It was time for Cassandra to get a real life. Besides, Beth needed the moral support.

"No. I'm perfectly happy with the way things are," answered Cassandra, making eyes at a particularly dangerous looking hottie at the bar.

"You've been cowering about Benedict for the last eight years. It's time you faced up to the past."

"I'm not seeing him again."

"That's not what I'm telling you to do. You'll never move forward with your life if you keep ducking the issue. You should confront him and move on."

"Tell me when you became the expert on 'unducking' the issue?"

"I'm learning. And you have to learn along with me because you're my friend."

"I'm not into self-improvement."

"You don't need to improve anything. You just need to stop treating men like Happy Meals, and you can't do that until you get over Benedict."

"I'm over Benedict," stated Cassandra flatly.

"And I'm secretly a porn star."

"There's no need for sarcasm."

"Oh, come off it, Cassandra. You've thrown over more men than anyone can count. Haven't you noticed the trend? Jessica, married. Mickey, married. The clock is ticking, my friend. Time is running out."

"You're still single," said Cassandra, looking smug.

"Not for long. I have plans. I'm going to find my perfect man and snap him up."

Cassandra tilted her head. "I thought you'd already found him."

"I don't know," Beth answered noncommittally, as if her heart wasn't already involved. As if she had a chance in hell of marrying the man she loved. "We're not getting any younger," she said quietly.

Cassandra pulled out her mirror and looked carefully. "I'm thirty-three."

Beth started to laugh when she noticed Cassandra examining the black hairs at her temples. "Find any gray?" she asked sweetly.

"Screw yourself, darling," said Cassandra, just as sweetly.

"Does that mean you're coming?"

"Under duress. But yes."

"You'll thank me for this someday," answered Beth as they ordered another round of drinks.

"If I don't murder you first," murmured Cassandra under her breath.

THREE DAYS LATER, Beth turned in her notice to Java4U, met Michael for a movie and then sealed the deal with her grandmother.

Beth's terms were firm. She didn't want a salary, but would take twenty-five percent of the post-tax profits. If there wasn't business, she wouldn't get paid. It was a risky proposition, but she wasn't going to be a charity case. She wanted to have a vested interest. She'd written about eight stories, which she thought she could sell, and that would get her through a couple of months of rent. After that, it was living on the whims of Earl Grey and cucumber sandwiches.

She hadn't heard from Spencer in the past few days, but she would see him the night of the benefit, and for that she had great things planned.

First off, it involved finding the perfect dress. Something classic and not tawdry, but sexy. She found a long black velvet gown, with a daringly wide-open neckline trimmed in silver. It was classic, would look good on her and at the same time would show the world that she had breasts. All in all, it was the right statement.

She wasn't worried because if Cassandra would be there as well, anything Beth wore would seem virginal at best.

Still, Spencer was going to notice *her*, whatever it took. Beth smiled to herself, already looking forward to the "whatever."

THE NIGHT OF THE BENEFIT came sooner than Spencer wanted. He alternated between hot-blooded bouts of anticipation and equally powerful fits of dread.

Beth expected him to be on his best behavior, and tonight he would be. He'd rented a tux and ordered a stretch limo. He'd considered flowers, but the more he thought about it, the more he hated it. Either a) he'd come off as insincere, because flowers weren't his style and she knew it, or b) which was even worse, he'd come across as trying to emulate the paragon of perfection, Michael Becket. And Spencer emulated no man.

When Beth opened the door to her apartment, he felt as if the floor had suddenly dropped out from beneath him. It was the same loss of gravity, the same loss of breath, the same heart-stopping fear.

For some reason, he'd never considered Beth a truly beautiful woman. Oh, she was sexy, charming and perky. But he'd never seen her looking sophisticated and cool—and dangerous.

"You ready to leave?" he asked, which sounded more like "Youreavyleave?" because he couldn't take his eyes off her chest, and his mouth was not functioning correctly.

"Sure," she said, a small smile playing around her mouth. She pulled the door closed and locked it with her key.

He didn't know if the limo was a smooth move or not. After one glance at the black stretch Town Car she shot him a questioning look. He just shrugged.

As he helped her into the vehicle, he took an extra few moments to admire her perfectly curved derriere as she wiggled her way down the long seat.

Then came the moment of indecision. Sitting dangerously close to her or safely at bay? She was looking at him with expectation; after all, this was a date. He would be expected to be near her, to touch her.

And he'd thought it would be easy. Ha. Of course, he'd been near her before, and except for that one big screwup, the touching hadn't been an issue.

Still, with her hair up in some sweeping chignon, diamonds winking in her ears and around her neck, and that cut-to-Australia neckline, not touching her was going to be damn near impossible. By the confident look in her eyes, he suspected she knew it, as well.

He sat across from her—and down a foot, so that their knees wouldn't brush in the close confines.

"Frightened of me?" she asked in a taunting voice, the cool siren once again.

"Terrified," he answered, and occupied himself with pouring a scotch, neat. "Drink?"

"No, thank you." She started to laugh. "Why do I frighten you? We've been out before. Hell, we've even had sex."

Quickly he pressed the button to raise the black glass divider between them and the driver. "Once," he said, needing to correct her.

She turned and met his eyes, hers flashing with banked desire. He gulped. "Once," she agreed. Then, from beneath the voluminous skirt, emerged a trim, shapely leg. A calf, a knee. God in heaven, a thigh! How far did that damn slit go? He scooted down a few inches.

The shoe began to bounce impatiently. And every third bounce she managed to brush those three-inch heels against his leg. He knew because his cock was throbbing right in time with her foot.

He coughed. "I think we need to clarify something. Set some boundaries for the evening," he said, his eyes permanently locked on the long length of thigh.

She shrugged. "Certainly. What boundaries were you considering, *mon petit chou?*"

Right now, his mind seemed occupied with the limitless boundaries of her legs. He shook it off. Business. Article. Legs.

"We'll just draw a line. Here. Now." He pointed to the silver seam in the floor carpet. "That's your side and this is mine."

"You really need to hide behind an imaginary barrier? Are you so afraid I'm going to pounce?"

She didn't understand that this was a matter of survival for him. "You can mock me if you choose, but I'm not changing my mind."

"Were you born this stubborn?"

"Don't waste your breath. Tougher than you have tried," he said, and folded his arms across his chest.

Slowly she shook her head. "All right." Then she looked at the silver seam, regret in her eyes. "This is my side?"

"Yes," he said, glad that she finally understood.

"Such a pity," she said, reaching behind her.

Then he watched as she unzipped the back of the flowing black gown. Watched as the creamy white skin emerged like a sea nymph climbing from her shell. She wasn't wearing a bra, so her breasts were suddenly there. Staring him in the face. Taut white flesh; round, pebbled nipples.

God in heaven. His body heated to throbbing steel.

But did she stop there? No, she was relentless, drawing the velvet down her legs and neatly folding it next to her as if her tidiness was at issue.

He refolded his arms across his chest. It was going to take more than cheap tricks to do him in. His eyes raked over her, looking his fill.

She had no panties, merely thigh-high stockings and killer heels. And a gleam in her eyes that said he was toast.

"What are you doing?" he asked, proud of the calm in his voice. He prepared himself for her touch, because he knew that was next. Hoped that he could resist.

However, her hand didn't reach out. Instead, she crossed one long leg over the other, stretched her arm out across the back of the seat. "I'm merely exercising my God-given right to sit nude in a limo. It's one of my favorite fantasies."

That was all he could take. His hand moved, a reflex reaction to having a beautiful woman sitting unclothed right under his thumb. His fingers stroked her knee, rode higher. For a moment her eyes closed and she sucked in her lower lip.

Then she opened her eyes and very coolly plucked his hand away. "Sorry. I forgot about those pesky boundaries. My bad."

She leaned down, her glorious breasts falling free, and he heard himself moan. "Your side," she said, drawing a toe down the line in the carpet.

Then she leaned back against the seat. "Mine. Since I'm not tough enough to change your mind." She tossed his words back at him.

It was a good forty-five minute drive to the Four

Seasons, and for Spencer, she might as well have pinned his privates on the rack. Forty-five minutes had never been so torturous.

Just before they arrived, she pulled on her dress, and he refused to admit he was disappointed. When he took his first step into the safe confines of the hotel, he scurried off to the nearest men's room to get rid of the most painful hard-on he'd ever possessed in his entire life.

8

Sadistic SWF needs man to inflict torture on. Serious torture. Only the most hardened of hearts need apply, because most of you peons are just going to be annihilated....

THEY TOOK THE ELEVATOR up to the Four Seasons lobby on the seventh floor, and then the stairs up to the Grand Ballroom. Everywhere they looked there were candles and poinsettias, and the side tables were decorated with artificial snow. It was a magical place for a magical night.

She had done it. He had thought she wasn't "tough enough." Ha. For the first time in her life, she was basking in a complete top-of-the-world experience.

Removing Spencer's hand had been painful, but she'd needed to teach him a lesson, and judging by the robust testament to her desirability in his trousers, he was learning it well. Although, when he came back from the men's room, the testament was substantially smaller. Self-gratifying coward.

He took her arm and smiled, once again in control. "Are you going to hide or do introductions?" he asked.

Beth, still playing the vamp, pressed his arm close to her breast. "Introductions."

Her heart was pounding so furiously she was positive her gown would give her away, but no one seemed to notice. She took Spencer down the line to meet her family, one by one. And who knew he could be so charming?

First, he complimented her mother on the good things the foundation had done for the town. Then when he spoke to her father, he slid easily into a business discussion of whether the current union environment was healthy for an industrialized city like Chicago. And when he got to *Grand-mère*, well, it was like Jekyll and Cary Grant. He was laughing at her old jokes, tuning out the rest of the world when he listened, and in general, making her fall in love.

When the band started up a waltz, Spence swept her grandmother up in his arms and whisked her out on the floor. And her grandmother actually blushed.

It stung Beth to realize she was jealous of a seventy-year-old woman. A blood relative, no less. But Spencer had walls he kept up. Big, high, impervious walls. And her grandmother just slipped right over them.

It was enough to make Beth scream. However,

she settled for drinking a healthy glass of champagne.

Eventually, it was her turn to dance with him, and she burst out with the question of the hour. "Who are you?"

"Spencer James."

Impatiently she brushed at his chest. "I know that. But what happened to your personality deficiency? Or is this some sort of special disorder where you hear the strains of music and it soothes the savage beast?"

"I think the quote was soothing the savage breast," he said, his finger skimming right down the middle of her chest. "Congreve, 1697."

At the evocative touch, she shivered. "Are you flirting with me?"

Immediately the openness in his expression switched off. Do not pass Go. Do not collect $200. "No. Sorry. Too much scotch."

They ended the dance in a much different space from where they'd begun it. As strangers.

As if the night wasn't bad enough, she heard a trilling voice that echoed in her head. "Spencer!"

Beth turned to see a handsome couple approaching, the dark-haired female vaguely familiar, but in a bad way.

"And this must be Beth! My, you haven't aged a bit in ten years."

Beth then realized the mystery woman's identity. "Joan Barclay."

Her old classmate from high school hadn't changed, either. The dark eyes were heavily made up, but it looked sexy, not trampish. The auburn hair was long and straight, shining beautifully in the bright lights. Only the mouth looked fuller. Collagen injections could do that, Beth thought to herself.

Joan pursed her chemically enhanced lips. "Actually, it's Joan James. Much more pedantic than Barclay, but, well, we don't choose how our hearts may fall."

Nothing could have prepared Beth for the knife that cut her in two. She sucked in a breath. "Your sister?" she asked hopefully.

"Ex-wife," said Spencer tightly.

"Oh," answered Beth stupidly because it was all becoming clear.

"I was so thrilled when Spencer said he was dating again."

"I've dated a lot, thank you very much. I just don't feel the need to flaunt my love life under your nose." He glared at his ex. "Unlike others."

The other gentleman, a tall, dark-haired, lanky man, seemed to take everything in stride. "She's a born flauntress. I'm sorry."

Beth smiled in gratitude. "Who are you?"

The gentleman held out a hand. "Harry Collingsworth."

"Nice to meet you," answered Beth automatically.

"He's my best friend," said Spencer in an oddly defiant voice.

"Dating your ex?" she said with a frown.

Spencer shrugged.

"And everyone's okay with this?" said Beth in confusion.

"Oh, yes," laughed Joan. "I've tried to make Spencer jealous for years, but failed miserably."

Harry leaned in. "They say he has no heart."

"If you're going to malign me, at least have the common courtesy to do it behind my back."

Joan stared. "My dear, I think we've done it. I think we've hit a nerve."

"Yes, well, after five years of drilling, I would think it would happen eventually."

Joan ignored him. "You know, he's mentioned you quite a bit. I had no idea that Spencer was getting involved again."

Beth stopped and stared at Spencer. "Well, you know, he keeps those secrets so well."

Then he wrapped an arm around her shoulders, although she suspected it was more to keep her in line than a gesture of affection. He wanted a pawn to keep his ex-wife guessing? Two could play that game.

She snuggled closer to him, feeling him tense. "Now that you've started, you've got me dying to know. What else has he said?"

Spencer coughed. "We don't need to do this."

Beth brushed a finger through his hair, delighting to feel him jump. "Oh, darling, I think we do."

"Spencer doesn't say much, merely stalks around cursing the world. It's just a hair more extreme than his normal bad temper, or I would have never guessed it. So how long have the two of you been together?"

"About six weeks now. Not long."

"That explains things," said Joan, smiling happily.

"What things?" asked Beth.

Harry interrupted. "Excuse her, Beth. She's speaking out of turn. Aren't you? There's some buried hostility that surfaces whenever you mention the divorce. Isn't that right, sugar?"

Joan pouted, but she quieted. "Yes, sweetums."

Spencer's hand began to stroke the curve of Beth's waist, shooting currents wherever he touched. She wondered exactly whose benefit this was for— Spencer's or Joan's? Beth visibly shivered, and it wasn't all for show. "Can you excuse us for just a moment? It's getting so hot in here."

She took Spencer's hand and dragged him to the bar behind the ballroom.

"Is this why you wanted to bring me here this evening? Just to show up your ex-wife?"

To his credit, he didn't bother lying. "Yes."

Noting the thunderstorm brewing on her face, he realized his mistake. "I did want to go with you."

"Oh, well, thank God for small favors," she said,

blinking furiously to keep the tears from welling in her eyes. There was absolutely no way he was going to make her cry.

She stiffened her jaw and rounded on him. "You've got sixty seconds to make this right. Now start talking and make it good."

She folded her arms across her chest, praying that he would.

SPENCER WINCED, for once wishing his natural-born talent for honesty would just go away. He led her over to one of the small tables in the bar. "Sit down," he ordered.

She obeyed.

"Now, I admit that my pride has been a little trampled on because of Joan and Harry."

"You're jealous?" asked Beth carefully.

"Jealousy would imply I would like to be in Harry's place, which I wouldn't," he declared, although why he needed to explain this to her, he didn't understand. The one thing he did understand was that he only knew that he couldn't stand the hurt in her face. "It's more complicated than that. I don't know why, but it bothers me."

"Maybe you still have feelings for her."

He laughed, but she didn't seem to understand why that was humorous. He tried another tack. "Look, if one of your friends began dating your ex, how would you feel?"

"Betrayed."

He held up a theatrical finger. "Exactly. And I admit that being here with you is a defensive maneuver, but I *do* want to be here with you."

"What do you want from me?" she asked.

He froze. "You're looking for marriage, a long-term relationship, and that's not what I'm in for. Been there, done that, and my 'personality disorder,' as you so aptly called it, really doesn't encourage me to walk down that aisle again."

She met his eyes, not backing down. "And you think that's all I'm interested in."

"Isn't it?" he asked, as all the noise in the room died away.

"That's my plan, yes. I'm going to find someone whom I can love and cherish for the rest of my life. But I haven't found anyone yet and I'm not involved exclusively, so if I chose to have a little fun, as it were, I don't think it'd detract from my plan at all."

"What are you saying?"

"No strings. There is an attraction between us, and there's no reason not to act on it. I can't pretend it doesn't exist and neither can you."

"Is this the new, liberated Bethany Von Meeter?"

She considered that for a minute, then met his gaze squarely. "Yes. It is. I can do this. I think. Isn't that what you want? Sex. No emotional involvement."

"I couldn't have an emotional involvement if I tried," he said.

"Then that's it. It'll be pure sex and pure sex only," she stated, her voice dropping to a whisper. Suddenly he was staring into the eyes of a seductress.

Spencer pulled at his collar, finding the room hot and crowded all at once. Her new image worried him. Bo Peep was safe. This woman in front of him, the one who earlier had stripped right before his eyes, scared the hell out of him.

So Spencer fought back the best way he knew how. "If you're thinking that you can sleep your way into marriage, you're wrong."

He never saw the glass of whiskey coming. *Wham.* Right in the eyes, and it burned like hell.

Quietly he pulled out his handkerchief. "I deserved that. I'm sorry."

"I warned you once. And there are no such things as second chances."

She glared at him, angrier than he'd ever seen her. Yet if she was angry, why offer him paradise? Something didn't make sense. "I want everything completely out in the open," he said slowly.

"You really want honesty? I've never met a man more in need of a heart transplant than you, and why you would even think I would want a relationship with you, other than a purely physical one, is beyond me. I have my pride, you know, and I'm sorry, but Michael Becket is ten times the man you are."

Oh, she knew how to kick a man right in the balls.

"Then why aren't you sleeping with him?" he retorted, because he needed to know.

Her smile was full of satisfaction. "Maybe I am. I told you, it'll be nonexclusive."

Spencer was going to destroy Michael Becket, one word at a time. No man touched what was his.

The wayward thought stuck in his head, and now it wouldn't go away. But this time, five years of defensive maneuvering had paid off, so he kept such foolishness to himself.

"You want sex, you got it," he agreed, but it left a bad taste in his mouth.

"Fine," she said, and got up out of her seat.

"Where are you going?"

"Back to the ballroom. I have real friends and family out there, and I'll be damned if I'm going to let you ruin this night for me."

Not knowing if he was heading for heaven or hell, Spencer followed.

BETH FOUND CASSANDRA almost immediately. In the midst of the crowded ballroom, she was hard to miss. Dressed in a red, low-cut, strapless number, she had a large percentage of the male population standing around watching her breathe.

She was talking to a tall, dark-haired gentleman who was, of course, devastatingly handsome.

Surprisingly, Spencer spoke first. "Noah?"

"Spencer!"

Spencer shook the man's hand and then explained to Beth, "Noah's my brother-in-law."

Then Beth saw the family resemblance—the thin face, the dark, flashing eyes. "Barclay? You're Joan's brother?"

Cassandra cleared her throat. "Excuse me, some of us would like introductions."

Then Beth realized that Cassandra had never met Spencer. "Cassandra, this is Spencer James."

Cassandra stared. "This is the journalist?" Immediately she took Beth's arm. "I need to freshen up, and so do you."

As she led her away, she whispered, "You didn't tell me you were bringing a date."

"It's not a date."

Cassandra opened the door to the ladies' room. "Did you come together?"

"Yes."

"Are you wearing perfume?"

"Yes."

"Coordinated lingerie?"

"That's none of your business," said Beth, blushing furiously.

"Aha! It's a date."

"Maybe it's a date, but there's no reason for you to get your nose out of joint."

"My nose is not out of joint. I'm fine." She sniffed. "Disappointed, maybe."

"Why?"

"I had this image of the two of us taking the ballroom by storm, but no—you've got a date."

"It's not a date," said Beth, taking shallow breaths. She was swimming in the deep end of the ocean now, and wasn't quite sure if she liked it.

"Look at you, wearing coordinated lingerie. First Jessica, then Mickey. It's only a matter of time."

Beth swallowed the hard truth. "I'm not marrying Spencer, so you've still got me."

"Oh, come off it, Beth. Look at that dress. How much did it cost you?"

"Five hundred seventy-nine bucks."

"Which is about your monthly income. This dress is a weapon of manly destruction, not a piece of fashion wear."

"He doesn't want to marry me. He just wants to sleep with me."

"Have you?"

"Once."

"And this is so you can make it to twice?" asked Cassandra, pointing to the dress.

Beth nodded. Spencer had been clear from the beginning he didn't do relationships at all. If they were to be together in any fashion, she was going to have to come over to his way of thinking, so tonight she had.

"I hope I did the right thing," Beth said, still not sure, but for once she was willing to do something a little less Von Meeter and a little more like Cassandra.

Cassandra gave her a reassuring hug, which was so unlike Cassandra that Beth looked at her suspiciously. "What was that for?"

"You're all I've got left. I'm savoring the moment before you're gone, too."

Beth elected to change the subject. "So what about Noah?"

"I found him by the caviar. He was eating Sevruga, but I liked him, anyway."

"I think he's gorgeous, but his sister is a total bitch," said Beth, checking to make sure her lipstick was in place. The night had been rockier than she'd expected, but her hopes were still high.

"You know her?"

"I went to high school with her. We used to play our friends against each other. Girl games. Nasty stuff."

"No way! I can't imagine you with your claws out."

Beth smiled as they walked out of the ladies' room. "You gotta watch the quiet ones, Cassandra. Always watch the quiet ones. We're the most dangerous."

WHEN BETH AND CASSANDRA made their way back to Spencer, it seemed Noah had disappeared to get drinks. Out of the corner of her eye, Beth spied Benedict O'Malley approaching, and judging from the steel rod that just replaced Cassandra's spine, she had seen him, too.

He was tall, broad, and had a chest like a boxer's. When he and Cassandra were living together, during Beth's last year at the University of Chicago, she had liked him well enough. Then when things started to fall apart, he became evil, not that he was truly evil, but fairly evil, because Beth was a loyal friend.

"Cassandra," began Benedict, "nice to see you."

"It hasn't been long enough," said Cassandra, not afraid to decimate a man in public.

"Can we dance?" he asked, a glutton for punishment. Still, Beth believed he deserved every bit of it.

"No," Cassandra answered coolly.

Spencer shot Beth a confused look. "Bad history," she muttered under her breath. Strictly because it was a fund-raiser and Beth was well-trained, she spoke up. "Benedict, very nice to see you. It's been such a long time," she said, with a polite yet frigid smile.

Obviously not as well-trained as Beth, Benedict never took his eyes off Cassandra. "Maybe a drink, then?"

"You're working in Chicago now?" Cassandra asked, and for just a moment the facade slipped.

"It's my home. I work for the city."

Noah approached, drink in hand. "O'Malley? Didn't expect to see you here."

Cassandra smiled sweetly at Benedict. "I'm sorry, we were just about to dance," she said, and pulled Noah out on the floor.

Beth noticed her mother signaling furiously, but was loath to leave her own personal soap opera. *In a minute,* she mouthed.

But the soap opera was over. Cassandra was cheek to cheek with Noah, and Benedict, poor Benedict, was left to watch. It was the first time that Beth had ever felt sorry for him. When you loved somebody, it could really, really hurt.

SPENCER TOOK ONE LOOK at the pained expression on the man's face and felt pity. "Women can be the very death of a man. Spencer James," he said, holding out his hand.

"Benedict O'Malley."

Beth tapped Spencer on the sleeve. "Give me just a minute. The parental unit seeks attention," she said, and then she turned and left.

"I'll be here," he said, and watched her go. Then he turned back to Benedict.

"Your ex?" Spencer asked, pleased to see someone who could screw up relationships even worse than him.

"Ex-girlfriend."

"Ah, an intelligent man."

"No. I should have married her."

"You could have just cut off your balls instead. Much less painful."

"I'm going to marry her. I made one mistake. Not going to do that again."

"You're the new set of eyes in the financial office.

Cleaning up after the kickbacks from last year," he said, already thinking of the angle he could use on the story.

Spencer watched Cassandra out on the dance floor. She was laughing and flirting and generally ignoring the man at his side. "She doesn't seem interested."

"She's just mad."

"Good luck," offered Spencer as he made his way over to find Beth. He spotted her laughing with her father, and there was such happiness in her face, something vibrant and alive. Happiness wasn't an emotion that Spencer had ever craved. He didn't like things messy, or disorganized, or out of place and emotions had always felt foreign to him.

Yet he couldn't deny that she invoked feelings in him, crumbs of pleasure and scraps of jealousy. Unfortunately, he didn't think it would be enough.

THE REST OF THE NIGHT passed by in a blur. Spencer was charming and attentive, and Beth realized that when he wasn't afraid of being trapped in a relationship, he was really quite irresistible.

As the evening wore on, the lights were dimmed and the great tree in the hall lit up in a fire of gold and silver lights. With Spencer holding her close in his arms, Beth decided it couldn't have been more perfect. Well, it could have, but she wasn't going to let herself think about that.

Purposefully, he steered her away from the

crowds, away from the hallway, away from the strains of music and laughter.

"How long do you have to stay?" he asked, his lips close against her neck.

Beth struggled to breathe. "Just a little bit longer."

He pressed up against her, and she felt his erection between her thighs, pressing urgently. "Why don't we go now?"

"I need to stay until the announcements at the end. My father will make a speech, and then I can duck out."

"When's his speech?"

Beth checked her watch. "About twenty minutes."

Spencer took her hand. "That'll do."

HE'D NEVER MADE LOVE in a limo before, had always thought it was tacky and juvenile, but he'd never been so desperate. All night long, he could only remember what she was wearing underneath her gown, remembering the white silk of her breasts, and he just couldn't stand it anymore.

He didn't wait to undress her, merely told the driver to go to the lakefront, then pressed the button to put the glass barrier in place. Minutes later he was inside her.

She sat astride his lap, her eyes burning, and he let himself drown in the indigo fire he saw in them.

"This is what you wanted," he reminded her, but really reminding himself. She'd given him carte blanche and he intended to take full advantage.

Her head fell back and he pulled the neckline aside, freeing her breasts. "Don't talk," she whispered. "Please. Just move."

So he followed her instructions. Not saying a word, merely pounding inside her as the streets of Chicago swept by. He should have felt relief that the strain of relationship talk was gone, an unpleasant diversion from two people's ability to simply enjoy themselves. However, something else was missing this time. Something wasn't quite right.

But soon he couldn't think anymore. Pleasure consumed him.

Just as their twenty minutes was up the car pulled over in front of the hotel. Beth tidied herself, Spence zipped his pants, and together they walked inside as if nothing had ever happened. It just seemed easier that way.

9

SWF needs spanking....

"SO THIS IS YOUR PLACE?" asked Mickey. She nodded her head. "It needs work."

Beth smiled, feeling the power course through her. "Damn straight."

"What do you know about bookkeeping?" asked Jessica.

"I took sophomore accounting," Beth said in her own defense. "And we hired a bookkeeper," she admitted quietly.

"Management?" asked Cassandra.

"I can handle that. It's not that different from Java4U."

Mickey began to laugh. "Boy, are you in for a shock."

It was their lack of confidence she resented most. "None of you think I can do it, do you?"

Silence.

"Some friends I have."

That started a flurry of discontent. "Now, Beth."

Oh, yeah, like words of comfort could make it all right. "Don't you, 'Now, Beth' me."

"Can we change the subject?" asked Mickey. "Before someone gets killed. Miss Cassandra, killed in the parlor, with the samovar."

Cassandra started to laugh. "Where did you get that monstrosity? You could live inside it."

"It's nineteenth century Russian. From Moscow." Jessica pursed her lips. "Ohh…"

"So, when is opening day?" Mickey asked as she pulled up a folding chair, which was only temporary until the real beauties came in. Hand-turned wood, with graceful legs.

"January second. One more month."

"Interviews done? Staff hired?" inquired Jessica.

The interviews had been the funnest part. However, Beth was going to surprise her friends with that one. "Got a few left to go through, but most are done."

"Sounds like you're almost there," said Jessica, and then glanced around the bare room. "Except for furniture."

"It's coming next week."

Mickey pulled out her PDA and started to write. "Cool. Opening, January 2. We'll be here."

Beth took note of the definitive "we." She wanted to be part of a "we," too. Unfortunately, progress on that front was slow to nonexistent.

"So what happened the other night? You disappeared." Beth turned to Cassandra, who was now her sole oar in the rough sea of coupledom.

"I left," replied Cassandra.

Beth raised her brow. "I figured that. With whom?"

Cassandra looked almost bored. "I was alone."

"What about Noah?" asked Beth, kind of curious if Mr. Construction Guy would walk on the wild side.

"Who's Noah?" asked Jessica.

"He's too uptight." Which only meant one thing. He'd turned her down.

Mickey looked at Beth. "Excuse me? Who is Noah?"

"He was at the gala," explained Beth. "You were busy."

"What's that supposed to mean?"

Beth picked up her pen, twirling it between her fingers. "I'm sure you had really important things to do on Saturday night, rather than attend my family's charity gala."

"Don't turn into Little Miss Diva thing. *You* missed it the past two years running."

Wow, it had worked for a moment. She felt powerful, take-charge. She'd been a real bitch. Beth smiled and put the pen down. "I don't want to hate you because you're married, but I have to be honest, it's very difficult sometimes to accept that you've crossed the line."

Now that she'd delved into this bitchy sort of honesty thing, it felt freeing. She tossed her hair.

"This is *so* not fair. I've been married for two weeks. That's *two weeks!* And there's stuff going on here that I don't know about. Men things that I have a right to know. Things that I would be party to if I were still single."

"Excuse me," interrupted Cassandra, "this is my personal life you are bandying about."

Beth put her hands on her hips and rocked back on her heels. "No, this is about a bigger issue than you getting shot down."

"She got shot down?" asked Jessica.

"We're optional now and it bothers me."

"I did not get shot down. Men do not shoot me down, thank you very much."

Beth watched the pen go round and round. It was almost hypnotic. "We're no longer required."

"That's not true," stated Jessica.

Beth wheeled on her. "And where were you on Saturday night, hmm?"

Jessica stuck her hands in her pocket, looking guilty. "Adam had a meeting with a client and I stayed home. I didn't know you were going. None of us did, except for Miss Single Cassandra. And even if I had known, I wouldn't want to go alone."

Wouldn't want to go alone. Because now she had that option. Beth's voice rose. "Did that stop Cassandra?

No. Now you're married, you can't go anywhere by yourself?"

Mickey raised her hand. "Excuse me. We're neglecting *your* evening. Did you go alone? And don't think that you can use the old I'll-go-on-the-offensive, but-ain't-nobody-talking-about-my-problems tactic. Which, by the way, you've never used before. Brava, Beth."

Beth bowed. "Thank you."

Mickey lowered her glasses. "So spill."

Beth wasn't spilling anything. Her spillage was messy and ugly and pathetic. "Actually, we're talking about Cassandra's problems."

"I do not have problems," insisted Cassandra.

Mickey shook her head. "He rejected you. That is so cool."

Jessica sneezed. "Nothing cool there."

"Rejection makes you human. Now I don't have to hate you anymore," said Beth, still going with the honesty thing.

"So who is Noah?" asked Mickey.

"Noah Barclay. He's into buildings, or something like that."

Beth started to smile. "I like him, even if his sister is a bitch."

"All you society types are just alike," snapped Cassandra.

"Oh come on, Cassandra," said Beth. "You're

usually a better sport than this. It wasn't anything personal."

"Well, since we're telling tales, what about your night?" Cassandra turned to Mickey and Jessica, *sotto voce.* "She's dating Spencer James."

It was so far from the truth that Beth felt like laughing. Or crying. "We're not dating."

"I thought you didn't like him?" asked Jessica.

Beth put the pen down. Honesty was no longer so exciting. That's what happened when it was directed at you. "I still don't."

Mickey raised her brow. "I see."

"No, you don't see. He's at a—" Beth wiggled her fingers, indicating quotation marks "—'bad place in his life.'" She stared out the glass front window, hiding from the astute eyes of her friends. "And on top of that, he's an ass."

"A very studly ass."

Beth shot a deadly glance in Cassandra's direction. "You're not helping."

"It's just payback, sweetie," said Cassandra, blowing an air-kiss in Beth's general direction.

"What about Mr. Perfect?" asked Mickey.

Beth thought for a minute, trying to remember who Mr. Perfect was. "I have a date with him on Tuesday," she said finally. They were going to have "the talk" soon. She could see it in his eyes. Michael had a nice amount of patience, but even Mr. Perfect had his limits.

"And Mr. Not So Perfect?" asked Jessica.

"I'm meeting him Wednesday morning."

Mickey raised a brow. "He's still going to do the article? Isn't that sort of, I don't know, unjournalistic?"

"His ethics are not his strength," said Beth quite honestly.

"Well, after all, he is a reporter," said Cassandra, who could find shades of gray in the darkest black.

Beth picked up her notepad and the Uniball pen and buried herself in her notes. "We're having sex, nothing more. A heartless affair."

"Well, if you say so," said Cassandra, sounding somewhat taken aback.

Beth smiled grimly without looking up. "Of course."

ON TUESDAY NIGHT SHE HAD that date with Michael. He was in high spirits, and it was contagious. They went to hear the Christmas performance at Symphony Center, and then afterward had hot buttered rum at Café Toulouse. He kissed her good-night and she noticed the way his dark eyes heated, but she feigned exhaustion.

"Thanks for a great night," she said with a platonic tap on his arm.

After he dropped her off at the door, she went inside and turned on the television. She had just changed into her pajamas when the phone rang.

"I need to reschedule our meeting tomorrow," said Spencer, without saying hello, or any other normal pleasantries.

"What time?" she asked, idly changing channels, not letting herself get excited or nervous, or beg him to come over.

"Can we do lunch instead of ten?"

"Sure. Is that all?" she asked.

He stayed silent for a moment. "Is he still there?"

Beth closed her eyes, wishing she could lie to him and say yes. "No."

He sighed audibly. "How did it go?"

Like he had a right to know. "Do you really expect me to tell you?"

"I have to write about this. What do you think?"

He always had an answer. Always the wrong answer. "Oh, I forgot. You're a journalist."

"Do you want to call this off?" he asked, and she paused, not sure what he was referring to—the article or the affair.

"No," she said weakly.

"Beth," he began.

She heard the need in his voice and it strengthened her own will.

"Good night," she said firmly and hung up.

THE NEXT DAY SHE MET Spencer at his apartment, a one-bedroom in Bucktown, not far from her own place. Somehow she had expected something more sophisticated.

He was still wearing a sport coat and tie, and she realized that he had come home from work. "You're at the office today?"

"Yeah. I had to turn in some copy. I need to be back in an hour."

A subtle reminder that she was never his first priority. "I could have just met you there," she said, pulling off her coat.

"No," he said, but he didn't elaborate.

Beth took the hint and sat down on the couch. "Have you eaten?" she asked, searching for idle topics of conversation. She was untutored in the art of tawdry affairs. *Love Slave: He Took My Body and Stole My Pride.*

"No, I wasn't hungry...." He slapped his forehead. "Are you? I could put something together...."

Obviously he was a novice, too. "No, don't worry about it." Her appetite had disappeared recently. "So, let's get down to work, shall we?"

He sat across from her and pulled out his pen and paper. All business. All the time. "Michael?"

"Yes. We went to the symphony."

"Did you like it?"

"No, not really," she answered, wishing they didn't have to talk about Michael.

He began to smile. "A House of Blues girl?"

She nodded. "Yeah. Heels just take all the fun out of music."

"Maybe we could go there sometime," he said, still meeting her eyes.

Now that was a new thing from him. It sounded almost as if he was asking her out. She tilted her head. "I'd like that."

Not surprisingly, he immediately changed the subject. "Any new bites on the ad?"

"Three good ones and twelve lewd propositions. That last one got a huge response."

He looked surprised. "Really?"

"Yes. I have four more dates set up, but I've scheduled them for after the holidays. I'm too busy to date. When is your article due?"

"Another week," he said, frowning.

"Great," she said, her hands primly in her lap. She'd only have a day or two left with him. If she set up a few extra dates with Michael before Christmas... No, she shot that idea down cold.

"How's the tearoom coming?" Spence asked.

"Good."

He grinned. "Have you hired all the waiters yet?"

"I've found seven, but most of the applicants aren't gorgeous enough."

"You're begging for a lawsuit," he said, shaking his head.

"Only if you tell."

"You're going to prove us all wrong, aren't you?"

he asked, with what looked like respect in his eyes...for the first time.

She warmed under that look. "What do you mean?" she asked, even though she knew exactly what he meant.

"It's going to be a smash, and you're just going to smile with that Bo Peep smile and say, 'I told you so.'"

She looked at him, surprised he knew her so well so quickly. "You think I'm that devious?"

"Of course you are," he said matter-of-factly.

For some time she watched him. "You like to read people, don't you?"

"I'm good at it. I dig inside their minds until I understand them."

"Has anyone ever interviewed you?"

He started to laugh. "No, I'm way too boring."

"You've been asked, though, haven't you?"

He shrugged, still ducking the question.

"Don't want anybody digging inside your mind, huh?"

He looked away and three times twirled his pen, studying it thoughtfully. "Do you have any more relevant details that the reading public needs to know about?" he finally asked.

End of subject. "No, that pretty much covers it."

"I still have about forty-seven minutes before I have to be back at work. You sure you're not hungry? We could get something to eat."

Beth saw the question lurking in his eyes, but questions weren't enough. She gathered up her coat. "I should go."

"Please don't," he said, his voice rough, the pen still. He didn't move, so she went to him. But today wasn't about power, today was merely two souls meeting in the middle, and for the first time, Beth truly began to hope.

THE NEXT FEW DAYS, she saw Spencer more than Michael. Most of the time she waited for him to call, but once she was feeling weak and phoned him late at night, ostensibly to ask about the next version of the ad, but mainly because she wanted to see him. Each time they were together, her body became more accustomed to him.

That night was the first time she stayed over at his apartment, and it felt oddly domestic. They watched television and then ended up making love on the floor. She could never keep her hands off of him, and thankfully, he seemed just as addicted. And Beth was learning to keep hope at bay.

The next morning, he offered her coffee as he dressed for work. "I'll be gone in minutes," Beth called from the shower. Using his soap, his shampoo, she savored his scent as she lathered her skin.

In the next moment, two hands appeared to help her, then a body, and then she was savoring much more than his scent. He touched her everywhere, and it was like it always was between them. Passionate and fast, with more anger than love.

She held fast to the wet tiles, clinging for support. And then he was spent, holding her close from behind. His hands touched her, pleasured her, and then she climaxed, as well.

Afterward, she pushed him away. "I need to finish rinsing my hair," she said, not daring to face him. He exited the shower just as quietly as he had appeared.

Then she turned her face to the warm spray and let the tears fall unchecked. And just as she'd promised, five minutes later she left.

SPENCER SPENT THE afternoon working the desk and answering the phone. The routine soothed him. Inside, it all felt wrong. The only time he felt at peace was when he was making love to Beth, and as soon as they were done, the guilt curdled inside him. This was her idea, he told himself over and over, needing to defend what they were doing. The words didn't seem to help. He knew that he needed to stop seeing her, but now it was too late and he couldn't.

Each time they were together, she turned further and further away. The woman he knew was vanishing before his eyes. When he made love to her, he began to work harder to please her, as if through her body he could win her mind. It didn't work. They would fall asleep exhausted, her body sated and full, but her mind remained closed and her smile appeared less and less often. He knew he missed it more and more.

The article was nearly finished, thank God, because he could no longer take her deifing Mr. Becket. What really drove Spence nuts was that when she spoke of Michael, she did smile. As if Spencer brought her pleasure, but Michael brought her joy.

Bastard.

THE FOLLOWING WEEK when she came over, Spencer had picked up Chinese food and a bunch of daisies. He didn't give them to her, just placed them in an old beer stein on his table, as if he enjoyed having them around. She didn't appear to notice.

That night he was rougher than usual, his hands more demanding. She responded in kind. Soon the two of them were locked in a battle, punctuated by his moans and her gasps. But Spencer wanted more from her tonight. He pleasured her with his mouth, his tongue, his fingers, tracing every inch of her flesh until she was begging him. However, tonight he was making her pay for so many things and he wouldn't let up. His tongue lashed inside her, finding the hard nub that guarded the only defenses he could breach. He suckled and pulled until her hips bucked furiously. Still he went on.

He loves her, he loves her not.

Then, she screamed. The sound brought no satisfaction to Spence, only sorrow. Far from feeling victorious, he rolled over to his side of the bed and stared into the darkness. Alone.

BETH KEPT THE PILLOW close against her chest. Her body felt worn and exhausted. Another time she might have wanted to stay the night, but now she needed desperately to leave.

The night of the gala, she had been so sure she could do this. She could be a liberal sophisticate, having her way with a man whom she wanted, but everything felt wrong. Every time he made love to her, she fell a little deeper under his spell, and yet he stayed the same as always. Passionate in bed, but remote everywhere else.

All this was wrong. She had thought she could do this, but she couldn't. It was time to get out.

She crept away from the bed and began to feel her way in the darkness. She had just pulled on her jeans when she heard him move, as well.

"Beth..." he began. And then Mr. Communicator stopped. She could sense him standing next to her.

"Here's your purse. Good grief, what have you got in this thing?" he asked, and then he dropped it. Right on her foot.

She tried to twist her foot out from under the heavy weight, instead she twisted it in a way that it was never meant to move.

She let out a yelp and fell back down onto the bed.

"Are you all right?" he asked, as he turned on the light.

"No," she said, and began to cry. Oh God, she hurt. Her ankle was killing her, she wasn't wearing her bra and he was never going to love her.

He pulled on a pair of sweats and took her ankle in his hands. "It's swelling up. I'll get some ice. I can take you to the hospital."

"No, thank you," she said, because his kindness was more than she could bear. "I can manage." She stood—oh, that was a bad idea—and then fell back again.

"I've got some extra-strength ibuprofen in the bathroom," he said, and then he disappeared. Eventually he returned, with a bottle of pills and a glass of water. "Take this. Do you need ice or heat?"

"How the hell should I know? I've never wrenched my ankle before."

He picked up the phone. "Who are you calling?" she asked, popping the pills into her mouth.

"The paper."

Was that really his entire life? "You don't have to miss work because I hurt myself."

He glared. "There's a nurse that works in the Tempo section. She works nights. She'll know what to do."

Beth felt only slightly ashamed. She pulled on her shirt. "I want to go home."

"You're not going anywhere. I'm responsible for this. I'm taking care of you. Besides, you're not going to be able to walk for a few days."

He held up a hand and spoke into the phone. After a short conversation, he hung up.

"Ice for twenty-four hours. Then heat after that. You have to stay off of it, keep it elevated. If it still hurts after three days, you see the doc."

"That all sounds very nice, but impossible. I have a tearoom that's opening up in exactly three weeks. Furniture is coming tomorrow. Special order. It's got to be unpacked and assembled. I have to be there."

"I'll cover for you."

"No."

He crossed his arms over his chest, looking stubborn. She felt the pills kick in, and the pain in her ankle numbed to a dull throbbing. He had a really nice chest.

"Let me do this for you. Please."

She knew that *please* wasn't a word that came easily to him, and every time he used it on her, her heartbeat raced.

"Two days, and I work remotely," she said, already feeling groggy.

"As long as it takes," he responded, and she had a feeling he wasn't talking about her ankle anymore.

10

Gimpy female doesn't really need a man right now....

WHEN BETH WOKE UP the next morning, the clock said 10:17 a.m. Spencer was long gone; she had vague memories of him saying something before he left.

She moved the covers aside and glared at the swollen mess that was her ankle. Weak, very weak. This time it was going to take more than a poor piece of muscle to keep her down. She put a foot on the floor and nearly cried.

No, no, no. Slowly the pain oozed into her system and she practiced her breathing, letting her body adjust. Not so bad, but pills would still help. After hobbling to the bathroom and taking medicine, she came back into the living room and dialed his cell phone.

"James here."

"It's Beth," she said, thinking of just saying, "It's me." But that would imply he would know who "me" was, and she wasn't ready to risk that. "Where're you at?"

"The tearoom. How's the ankle?" he asked.

"Hurts like hell," she said with gritted teeth, noticing he had no Christmas decorations at all. There were so many things she needed to do, she had to call Jessica next....

"Are you standing on it?" he asked.

Quickly she sat down. "No."

"Good. Keep it elevated. There's a heating pad at the end of the couch. I got it this morning. Healing Heather said that you should be okay if you keep off of it."

"Healing Heather?"

"It's a column she writes. We call her that."

"Sounds like a fun bunch."

"It pays the bills," he said, as if he didn't really love what he did. She knew better.

"Has the furniture come in yet?"

"Uh-huh. I'm almost done unpacking and then I'll do the assembly."

"You can do that?" she asked, realizing she knew little of what he was capable of.

"Yes, I can do that."

She hugged the throw on the couch tighter. What a difference six hours could make. Last night, she'd been cursed with the last embers of a relationship, now she had an ankle that was three sizes too large, and a man who seemed intent on making himself indispensable. "Thank you. I'll owe you big."

"No, you won't. Consider it my way of thanking you for the article."

"Goodbye, Spencer," she said, hanging up. *Thanking her for the article.* Yeah. God forbid we bring anything personal into it.

HARRY STUDIED THE PILES of boxes and packing materials, searching for Spencer. "What is this mess?"

Spencer ignored the rhetorical question and kept working. He couldn't spare a minute. "Did you pick up my notes?"

Harry handed him the papers. "Here."

In return, Spencer handed him a screwdriver. "Here."

"What is this place?" said Harry, staring in confusion at the screwdriver.

Spencer peered up from under the table he was currently working on. "If you're going to talk, at least work and talk. Don't start with the tables, they're a nightmare. Do the chairs first."

Harry began to unpack a box.

Spencer sighed. "No, those over there," he said, pointing to the five orderly piles he'd made in the corner. "They're ready to go. Start with the left front leg, then the back right, move to the—"

Harry cut him off. "I think I can do this myself. I took wood shop in junior high."

Spencer went back to work. Now he'd wasted a

good three minutes arguing. He'd never get this done in time. "It's going to be a tearoom."

Harry looked up in shock and Spencer gestured for him to keep working.

Harry put a leg in place. "So, you have a new business. What the hell are you doing?"

"It's not mine. It's Beth's."

"Oh," said Harry, and then fell silent.

"It's not what you think," said Spencer, because he knew exactly what Harry was thinking. It was what anyone would think. She was staying with him—only until her ankle healed, of course. It was guilt that made him insist. Guilt, of course.

Harry shrugged. "I like her."

Spence didn't look up. "So do I."

For a while Spencer stayed quiet, putting together one point two tables. When he checked his watch, he swore. "How much time can you spare today?"

"How much do you need?"

"I've got twelve hours to assemble eighty chairs and thirty tables." He checked his watch. "I've got chair assembly down to twelve minutes and I've clocked a table at forty-six minutes—those legs were made by the devil."

"How many extra man hours are required here?"

"About seventeen," Spencer admitted, picking up the screwdriver and tightening the last screw.

Harry started to laugh.

"It's feasible," Spencer said defensively. But only

if he cloned himself for the extra five hours. Still, he promised Beth that he'd do this for her and he would.

"When's the dating feature deadline?" asked Harry.

"Next week."

"Are you going to see her after that?"

Spencer set the table upright and examined his work. Perfect. "No," he said quite calmly.

"Oh."

Spencer noticed that Harry was slacking again. "Can you pick up the pace?" he asked, pulling out the next table.

"Why don't you just ask her out again?"

"She messed up her ankle and she'll be down for a few days," he said, as if that would prevent him from dating her. Of course, she had a date with Michael the Singer in two days, so the argument really didn't hold water.

"What happened to her ankle?"

"I dropped her purse on it."

"That seems like an extreme injury for a purse."

"Actually, she twisted it pulling it out from under her purse. Since she started working here, she's been carrying tools around and it was really heavy."

Harry began to laugh.

"Get back at it," growled Spencer, pulling out the

next table. He'd done the last one in thirty-eight minutes. If he worked just a little faster...

"So now merely rejecting the woman isn't enough. You maim her as well."

Spencer attacked the leg, putting it in place and screwing it tight, nearly stripping the threads in the process. "That's enough."

"Oh, all right."

A few minutes later Harry spoke up again. "I need to talk to you about something."

"What is it?"

"I've asked Joan to marry me, and this time she said yes."

Spencer stopped and wiped his brow. "Can't you elope? I could use the extra fifteen hundred a month. Maybe I'll buy a new car."

"Why don't you just make peace with her? She'd let you off the hook if you would just be polite to her."

Spencer twisted the screwdriver tighter in his hand. "Losing the fifteen hundred a month is easier."

"I'm in love with her."

Spencer put down his tools. "I know. She loves you, too, in that twisted, sadistic manner that makes her so special."

"She's really not that bad."

"I know that, too. I was married to her once."

"My life would be much easier if the two of you could act amicable."

"Didn't she tell you? I'm a heartless bastard with an EQ of ten. It's not in my genetic makeup to live amicably with another person," Spencer said, twisting the screw just a bit harder.

"How the hell did the two of you ever make it to the altar?"

"It took three weeks and a case of scotch."

Harry shook his head. "You know what your problem is?"

"You're going to tell me, right?"

"You're impulsive and you hate it."

"I'm not impulsive."

"Marrying someone after two weeks?"

"I've learned from my mistakes."

"Would Beth be another mistake?"

Spencer picked up the hammer, his face carefully bland. "This is about you and Joan."

"Oh come on, Spencer. How long have you known her?"

"Three weeks now." He'd first seen her on the twenty-seventh of November at exactly 9:47 p.m.

"Do you love her?"

Spencer moved to the back of the table, trying to work, trying to concentrate. He'd asked himself that same question over and over, but he had little faith in his level of feelings, such as it was. All his life, he had been reserved and restrained. His one experiment into relationships had been a failure, and he wasn't willing to hurt Beth. "You need to get back to work. I'm never going to finish."

Harry started putting on the chair back completely wrong, but Spencer kept his mouth shut.

After he finished the table, Spence looked up from his work. "Harry, congratulations. I do mean it."

Harry kept on hammering away. "I know. Get back to work."

JESSICA WAS THERE in record time with clothes, Christmas decorations and the insurance papers that Beth needed to fill out.

"I'm going to pay you for this. And your time, too. Look at all this stuff."

Jessica had outdone herself, producing three shopping bags full of garlands and ornaments and even a little tree.

"It's all here. Everything you asked for. So what's on the agenda today?" Jessica asked.

Beth pulled out the tree and hobbled over to set it up on Spencer's desk. "I need to find a plumber, arrange phone interviews for the last seven applicants and finalize my advertising budget."

"And the Christmas decorations? What's with that?"

Beth held up her hands. "Look at this place. It needs help."

Jessica sat down on the chair. "Sit down. Why are you here?"

Beth obeyed, but took the bag of ornaments with her. "I don't know. It seemed like a good idea at the time."

"That was before you hurt your ankle?"

Beth nodded. "I'm giving up."

"Fallen into the I-can't-change-him phase? Take your losses and move on. If he was any sort of decent man, he'd be here taking care of you."

"That's not fair. He's called twice already to just check on me, though I did call the first time. But he's at the tearoom. The furniture has arrived and he's helping."

Jessica smiled. "Cool. That's worth points."

"Yeah, but unfortunately, furniture assemblage does not a relationship make." She had actually analyzed that, which said something about her state of mind, although she liked to blame it on the medication.

"Some men just can't cut it, Beth. They're just not relationship guys, and you're a relationship gal. Besides, there's a lot of fish in Lake Michigan. You've met a lot."

"Michael. He's nice. He's more than nice. Why can't I love him?"

Jessica smiled. "Don't be sad. Maybe you can. Have you tried?"

Beth pushed her hair back and propped her ankle up on the couch. "Not really."

Jessica got up and slapped her on the leg. "Okay, let's get to work. How long are you here?"

"Three days."

"Good. You'll be home by Christmas Eve. My advice? Forget Mr. James when you leave here. Go home and set up a nice, cozy, romantic evening with Mr. Perfect. You need closure and you're not going to get it here."

Jessica was her most practical friend, and that was what Beth needed today. "You're right. Let's get to work. Can we start with the Christmas decorations?"

Jessica just glared.

WHEN SPENCER GOT HOME that night, the first thing he noticed was the tree. It wasn't a big one as far as Christmas trees went, not that he was an expert. He was allergic to pine, so he'd never bothered.

At first sniff, it smelled like real pine, but it was cold plastic to the touch. Then he spied the can of genuine pine scent hidden behind the tree. It was the kind of detail that only Beth would care about. But it did smell nice.

The colored lights winked in the darkness, and he found himself smiling. On the top, she'd put an angel. Figures.

He walked over and picked it up. She had blond

hair pulled up behind the high cheekbones and wide blue eyes. It was just like Beth, and she'd probably never even noticed. Of course, ninety percent of Christmas angels probably looked like her and she wouldn't notice that, either.

If she had gone out and hobbled around town, just to indulge her Christmas habit, just for him...

Under the tree was one small box. She'd wrapped it with newspaper and a shoelace. Softly, he laughed. Then he picked up the box and shook it. It was quiet. Next he sniffed carefully. No obvious scent. Not cologne. Maybe a tie, but it was really too short for a tie. He started to slide a finger beneath the newsprint, but decided to wait instead. He bet that she opened all her presents on Christmas Day.

He glanced over and realized that she was sleeping on the couch, a notepad clutched to her chest. At least it wasn't the power sander. For a minute he stood over her, watching. It was turning into a habit with him, looking at her while she slept. It was the one time that he could watch her possessively and dream.

She sighed in her sleep, and he bent down and picked her up. Bo Peep shouldn't sleep on couches, only in beds. He pulled the blanket over her, and quietly undressed. Then he settled himself on the couch. He lay awake, watching the lights on the tree, wondering about the one small package, and he fell asleep dreaming of the angel on top of his tree.

11

SWF looking for a man with a heart....

THERE WEREN'T MANY buildings in Chicago more spectacular than the offices of the *Chicago Herald*. There was history here and you felt it when you walked beneath the shadow of the gothic spires. Spencer had worked at only one place after getting out of college, and it was the only place he ever wanted to be.

Today he had a morning meeting with the Tempo editor to discuss the Internet dating article, which was set to run in the Sunday edition of the paper. Then his brief foray into the life of Bethany Von Meeter would be complete. He frowned, more heavily than usual, and told himself it was because he hated meetings with Edna.

Spencer entered her office, eyeing the walls covered with photographs and gossip columns. And then there was the smoke that filled the air when you walked into the room, the haze thicker than witch's brew.

Edna Hunter Gunter was fifty-three years old but

didn't look a day over ninety. She had the raspy voice of someone who thought filtered cigarettes were for wimps. However, Edna knew what would sell. Since she'd come on board, the lifestyle section had undergone a complete makeover and the advertising revenues were growing substantially. So management overlooked the fact that Edna believed in her constitutional right to smoke, even in a non-smoking building.

While he waited for her to show up, he noticed the magazines on her desk. *Vogue, Vanity Fair, True Fantasies.* Spencer laughed and picked up the latter.

As he thumbed through the magazine he noticed a familiar name, or an almost familiar name. Beth Von Masterson.

"I live in the big city of Chicago...."

He heard the hacking cough of Edna approaching, and he slipped the magazine underneath the stack of papers he had in his hand.

Then she swooped into the room, a cloud of smoke trailing behind her. Spencer waved a hand through the dense air and coughed.

"Spence, it's good, but I think we could do a little more with it."

It was demeaning to hear criticism of his work from someone who studied shoes for a living, but he had purposefully watered down his writing for this assignment. He didn't want to hurt Beth by being artificially harsh, he didn't want to encourage her, either. So "bland" was the angle he was going for.

"What do you want me to do?" he asked.

"Tell me the details about the subject of the article. I felt like we really didn't know her. Usually your work is much better than this. I didn't understand what drove her to this dating of the last resort," Edna said, her fingers tapping on the desk.

"There's not much to say," Spencer offered in his own defense. "What do you want to know?"

"Not me, our audience. She's not interesting. Liven her up, give her a personality, give us the details of who she is so that we actually want to read about her."

Mechanically, Spencer began reciting the facts. "She's twenty-eight years old, college grad from U of C, majored in English, couldn't find anything, so she's moved from job to job for the past few years."

"Bor-ing. Give me something more. What does her family think of the dating?"

Now was the time to hedge. "They don't know."

Edna's eyes widened. "Ah. They wouldn't approve, would they?"

Spencer shook his head. "No."

"Conflict, my boy. It's the heart of the story. What's the conflict here? Girl of the lonely hearts strikes out on her own, keeping it a secret from Mom and Dad in order to find the man of her dreams, which, by the way, if she ever did find a match, she'd introduce as the man she met at church, rather than via a computer. There's your story. She hasn't found a match yet, right? Maybe we should follow the story all the way through to the end. This one date sounds like he's it. We could wait and see."

Spencer closed his eyes. The singing Becket was more than he could handle. "No. Besides, she might never find the man she wants." After all, when a woman set her standards too high, she was doomed for failure.

"Good point. Okay, why wouldn't the family approve?"

"They're very strict. Her father hates computers. It's a mess," Spence lied.

"In this day and age? Oh, that's good."

"No, we're not writing about it."

"So what's the conflict, then? Why is this interesting?"

Spencer took back the article, the whitewashed, homogenized words he'd written. He'd shaped it to protect her as well as himself. "She's afraid of being alone."

"Woman nears thirty, driven to desperate means in order to find love? Great!"

"Her friends are all getting married," Spencer added.

"No one to go shopping with anymore? Can we

play up this angle? That would have some resonance."

Spencer stood up, paper in hand. "I'll see what I can do," he said. "About those lunch expenses. I thought they would be covered."

Edna tapped her cigarette pack against her desk. "Sorry. I went to bat for you, kid, but I was overruled. Damn bean counters."

She was lying through those tobacco-stained teeth and they both knew it, but in another two weeks he'd be out of there.

"Oh, Spence. Got another assignment for you."

"I'm going back to hard news," said Spencer, ready to give notice if she balked. The terms of the bet with Harry said that Spencer would spend only a month in the Tempo section. Marge would be back from maternity leave and he'd be back covering his normal beat.

"You're mine until New Year's. One more assignment."

"What about?" Spencer asked as he opened the glass doors.

"Santa Claus."

"Excuse me?"

"Santa Claus. We're doing an article on the fake Santas in the city. What drove them to being Santa, what do they get out of it? A feel-good, Christmas spirit sort of piece."

"Except that you're also telling the world that

Santa Claus doesn't exist," said Spencer, having a pseudo out-of-body moment, amazed that he was even arguing this.

Edna lit up another cigarette. "Nah. We're not going to do a hatchet job on Santa. More just a profile of the Santas of Chicago."

"I don't think I'm right for this one."

"What? You're perfect. You're not blinded by the sentimentality of it all. No schmaltz or violins. If Santa's doing heroin, I want it in there, and I know you'll write it."

Spencer nodded once. "All right. When do you want to run it?"

"Christmas Eve."

"Sure," he said, racing out before Edna decided they needed a feature on the tooth fairy, as well.

BETH HAD PUT HER FOOT down—her good one—and made Spencer take her to the tearoom. She spent most of the morning asking questions as the contractors came in and out. The plumber had installed a sink and industrial dishwasher in the back. The carpenter had fixed the hole on the side wall of the wooden bar, the glass man had installed the bar-length mirror and the flooring man had brought in the Persian carpets, rolled up now in front of the bar. She had put her stamp on the place, not even realizing that she had one. After looking around, she knew that she approved.

About lunchtime, her foot started to ache, so Beth propped it up on a chair and popped some more ibuprofen. There was one last wait-staff interview in an hour, and she hoped that this hottie fit the bill, because she was running out of gorgeous Chicago men. Actually, most of them were boys.

"What are you doing?" a deep voice snapped from the doorway.

Beth didn't bother to glance up. "I'm working. I have one interview left and then I'm going home."

"I can do it."

She rolled her eyes. "I don't think so."

"Why don't you put it off until tomorrow?" Spence hung his coat on the new coatrack near the door and came over to look at her foot.

"It's fine and I'm not going to put off the interview."

"Have you eaten?"

"I had a bagel earlier," she said, thinking it'd only been a quarter of a bagel left over from the day before, but that counted.

"Where's your coat?"

"I'm not leaving. I have an interview in an hour."

"We'll be back before then."

She sighed, thinking how well he fit here. If he'd let her slap a tux on him, she'd have her last waiter. A great idea, but she didn't relish near-death experiences, so she grinned instead. "It's in the back."

He stalked to the kitchen and returned with her old woolen jacket. "You should get a new coat."

"No, thank you. That one's lucky."

"Whatever. Here." He helped her into it and then slid an arm around her waist. "I got a cab right outside."

While lunching at the little bistro around the corner, Beth spent time checking out the competition.

"Do you think this is good?" she asked, watching while Spencer devoured his pasta al dente.

He looked up. "You don't like your chicken? Do you want to go someplace else?"

She lowered her voice. "No, I just want to know what a cultured consumer thinks of the restaurants in the area."

He slowly nodded. "Ah. You're going to kick their butt."

Beth sat up straighter. "Really?" She'd never been a butt-kicker before.

"Are the chairs and tables okay?" he asked, not looking up.

"Absolutely. Thank you."

"It was nothing. Anything else you need?"

She shot him her seductive businesswoman look. "What other skills do you have?"

He put down his fork. "I can do some of the electrical work. I can do the re-tiling in the kitchen if you want."

"I was making a joke."

"Oh," he said, and then went back to attacking his food. "The article's running in Sunday's paper," he murmured between bites.

"Really? Oh, I can't wait to read it!"

She'd never been "officially" in print on her own before. Always as the daughter of Charles Von Meeter, or granddaughter of social grande dame Muzzy Von Meeter.

"By the way," Spence said casually between bites, "I read your story."

"What story?" she asked.

"An Affair with the Mob. My Lover Was a Made Man."

Beth swallowed. Well, okay, the planets were lining up a little differently today. "Did you like it?" she asked, preparing herself for the worst.

"It wasn't bad. A little overdone, but I think that's to be expected. Why are you doing it?" he asked, staring at her intently.

"Money," she said, with more of that I-can-be-a-bad-person honesty.

"You could get a job at a respectable place."

"No. It was a way to pay some bills. Nothing more. I've got a story coming out in the November issue, too. But I don't want to be a writer—like you."

"What do you want?"

"Something that's my own." She would never be a trailblazer like Jessica or Mickey, and she would never do cool artsy stuff like Cassandra. Sometimes she just felt lost when she compared herself to everyone else, but now she was beginning to feel found.

"The tearoom?"

"If it works out." If it didn't, then she didn't know if she could try again, which was a depressing thought, and she didn't like depressing thoughts, so she changed the subject. "I can't wait to buy the paper to see what you've done."

He stopped and looked at her, puzzled. "You don't want to read it before it goes to print?"

"Well, no, that would spoil the fun of it."

"But you don't know what I've written."

"I trust you," she answered, wanting to believe in him.

"You're too naive," he said, carefully folding up his napkin and putting it neatly at the side of his plate.

Now Beth was getting nervous. "Why? Did you write something I should be worried about?"

"No," he answered, honest words from a man who wouldn't know rose-colored glasses if they fell off his nose.

"Okay. What's your point?"

"My editor wants me to play up the aging bachelorette angle, the victim of the ticking clock."

Beth's appetite died. "I see. Well, that'll make me

the big loser then, won't it?" Sometimes the world wasn't really rose-colored, after all.

He met her gaze. "No. I wouldn't do that. I made some changes this morning. You can read them."

No. She had to gamble on this one. More than that, she had to gamble on him. "I don't want to sit on your shoulder and be Madam Censor cracking her whip. This is up to you."

"I'd really feel better if you read what I wrote before it's printed," he said, and it was the first time she'd seen him uncertain.

However, for Beth, the matter had already been decided. Kicking butt, taking no prisoners was now the order of the day. Throw the sharks into the ocean and see what sort of articles they would write. She checked her watch. "I have to be back at the tearoom in three minutes."

A smile played at the corner of his mouth as he put some money on the table. "I'll get a cab."

"They'll never get here in time," she said, grabbing her coat and opening the door.

"Damn it, Beth."

Before she could stop him, he had picked her up and was carrying her in his arms.

"I can walk," she said in her best taking-no-prisoners voice.

"Too bad," he said, missing the whole kicking butt, taking no prisoners tone.

As soon as they got back to the tearoom, he deposited her in a chair. "After the interview, you leave, and tomorrow you stay home."

She sat up a little straighter, adjusting her shirt and slacks. Her foot was starting to smart painfully and a heating pad would feel really nice about now. She gave him a mutinous stare. "If you're lucky."

"Don't argue."

He planted a quick kiss on her forehead and then he left.

It was a good thing he didn't turn back, or he might have caught her smile.

SPENCER SPENT THE REST of the afternoon covering his old beat. In between a meeting with the mayor and a talk with the city planning office, he added more editorial changes to the dating article.

And why wouldn't she read the damn thing first? Instead, he was facing some honorability test. Spence shuddered in horror.

"Not moonlighting today, I see," said Harry, pulling up the extra chair at Spencer's desk.

"No. Today I earn my living."

Harry held out his hands. "I got blisters yesterday. Did you know that? Joan wanted to know what rock I'd been climbing."

"Did you say anything?"

Harry shook his head. "Not my place, and I didn't want to hand her any more ammo."

Spencer went back to work. "Thank you for small favors."

"So what's she going to call the restaurant?"

"No idea, but she's got ads to place and the sign has to be ordered by next week."

"It needs to be something high-class, something that symbolizes old money."

Spencer thought for a minute. "Nah. Something a little less formal." And he thought of Beth. "But still classy," he added.

"Bethany's."

"I like it. I'll tell her later."

"Finished with the article?"

"I hope." Spencer moved his monitor so Harry could see the screen. "If you read that, would you want to kill me?"

Harry quickly scanned the text. "It's good. But if she reads it, she'll know."

"Know what?"

"That you love her."

Spencer knew when he was being conned. "There's nothing in here to indicate that. I don't write claptrap."

Harry picked up his baseball cap and put it on backward. "See? You don't deny it. She'll figure it out."

"I'm not in love with her, and she won't figure it out."

"Whatever you say, champ. Want to grab a beer?"

"No, I need to get home as soon as I finish up here."

"Little woman waiting for you?"

"Yeah," said Spencer, and his heart warmed like a man in love. This time he shook it off.

THE NEXT MORNING WASN'T much to write home about. Beth still kept alive her secret hopes that Spencer would fall on his knees, confess his undying love, and they'd ride off into the sunset together. Spencer didn't seem to be following that train of thought. Instead, he made her breakfast—a very good omelette, made her drink two glasses of orange juice—she argued that vitamin C would not heal a twisted ankle, and finally noticed the decorations—promising severe punishment if she had actually gone shopping for "overcommercialized doodads"—his words, not hers.

As he was leaving, she brought up the question of her going home. Her home. Back to her apartment. He stuck a cup of hot coffee in her hand, told her that he'd be working late and walked out the door.

Relationship by denial.

After four hours of phone interviews with very nice sounding waiters, she scanned the messages on her answering machine. Michael had called. "I want to go away with you. Someplace for a long weekend where we can be alone. Sleigh rides and long nights in front of the fire..."

Beth closed her eyes, imagining Spencer saying those very words, knowing that he'd have bamboo splints under his fingernails first. A part of her acknowledged the fact that had she met Michael first, she'd probably be head over heels. In love with love.

Maybe her feelings for Spencer had just come from loneliness. Oh, yeah, that was good. More likely her feelings had come from a self-punishing desire to feel disappointment.

She wanted to believe in him and have enough confidence in herself that she could make it work. However, self-confidence wasn't something that gushed through her veins.

She called Michael back and almost told him that she had hurt her ankle, but thought better of it. Instead, she just said that after the holidays the sleigh ride sounded perfect.

THE PAPERWORK WAS GOING to be the death of her, but so far everything on Beth's checklist was getting checked off. Major progress.

Insurance? Check.

Department of Public Health inspection scheduled? Check.

Ads placed? Check.

Spencer? No check.

Time to cut her losses, she figured, just as Jessica had said. Tomorrow she was going home.

Just then the buzzer sounded, and Beth limped over to see who had arrived. "Yes?" she called.

"Oh, I'm sorry. I was ringing for Mr. James."

Beth winced, recognizing Joan's voice. "He's not here."

"Who are you?" asked Joan, even though Beth knew that Joan knew exactly who she was talking to.

"Cleaning lady," she lied, just to spite her.

"I didn't think Spencer could afford a cleaning service. It's you, isn't it, Beth?"

"Got me."

"I'll come up and wait. It'll be fun to catch up on old times."

"Joan, we hated each other in high school," said Beth, letting the cold, hard truth roll off her tongue.

"Well, yes, but surely we can let bygones be bygones."

Beth tapped her fingers against the wall panel, weighing her options. Spencer would have told Joan to go jump in front of a bus. However, Beth was not Spencer, and had been brainwashed with way too many lectures on good manners, so she pressed the button to open the door downstairs.

A few minutes later, Joan Barclay James waltzed into the room with an elegant cape and a wave of perfume.

Cheerfully, she threw an air-kiss at Beth and settled herself on the sofa.

"Scotch," she commanded, while pulling off her gloves.

Beth trailed into the kitchen and poured a double scotch for Joan and a glass of water for herself.

Joan smiled as she took her drink. "So."

Beth pushed her hair from her eyes. "So."

"I shouldn't be drinking. I haven't had a bite to eat all day," said Joan, taking a large mouthful of scotch.

Yeah, anorexia will do that to you, Beth mused. Of course, Spencer would have been proud of her for the thought, even though she hadn't said it aloud.

Beth smiled and raised her glass. "Cheers."

"What did you do to your foot?"

"Twisted the ankle. It's almost healed."

"Ah. Poor dear. So sorry."

"S'all right. You wanted to talk?"

"Oh, don't be nervous. I'm not going to subject you to the third degree or anything. I think it's wonderful that Spencer is moving on."

"Moving on is good," said Beth, staring at her empty ring finger.

"Isn't it, though? I'm going to be shopping for *my* ring soon. Just need to find one that's absolutely to die for," said Joan as she was clearly scanning the place.

"So you're moving on as well," prompted Beth. Anything to avoid talking about Spencer.

"Yes, Harry. He was a good friend during the divorce. Nasty business, and when it came time to divide up the assets, I picked Harry."

"He seems very nice."

"After Spencer, it's like night and day." She clapped a hand over her mouth. "Oh, I shouldn't have said that, should I?"

The buzzer sounded again, and Beth buzzed her up.

Muzzy Von Meeter had arrived.

"Do I know you?" Muzzy asked, while Beth took her mink coat and hung it up.

Joan stood. "Joan Barclay."

Muzzy nodded. "Yes. Are you a friend of Bethany's?"

"We attended school together, but I was actually here to see Spencer."

"Ah, yes, Mr. James. And where is he?"

"Working," said Bethany, wishing she felt less trampish. But there was something distinctly non-Von Meeter about being in a man's apartment when he wasn't there.

"I see," said her grandmother, nodding.

Joan's posture straightened up as she met Muzzy's disapproving gaze.

"So, what are you here for, if Spencer's not?"

"He's my ex-husband," said Joan, her shoulders slumping just a bit.

"Failed, did you? I've been married to Harold for fifty-seven years. It takes patience and care to make a marriage work. I suppose some have it and others don't."

"Yes, well, you've never been married to Spencer."

Beth smiled. Yes, she hadn't been married to Spencer, either. And it looked like she'd never get her chance to fail as well.

Joan eyed Muzzy, then looked at Beth, and stood. "I think I'll go."

Muzzy feigned disappointment. "Oh, but I was so looking forward to a chat."

Joan shook her head. "Too much to do. I have a wedding of my own to plan and it's going to be fabulous. I can't spare another minute."

"What did you need, *Grand-mère?*" Beth asked, choosing to ignore Joan.

Muzzy pulled a pair of glasses from her purse and handed her an envelope. "My lawyers couriered this over. It's the last of the documents on the incorporation. You should be able to file for the tax certificate now."

"Thank you. I was waiting for this."

"I called the tearoom yesterday when you weren't answering your phone at home."

Beth raised her eyebrows. Spencer hadn't said anything.

"Mr. James told me you were staying while you're incapacitated. Very gallant."

Gallant wasn't exactly the word Beth would have used, but she nodded anyway.

Beth heard the sound of a key in a lock. Not exactly the quiet evening she had envisioned where she could finally lay everything on the line. It was going to be her final ultimatum.

"Your mother will be here tomorrow," Muzzy announced, just as the door opened.

Beth's stomach did a big uh-oh, but she smiled bravely. "I'll call her. There's really no need for her to visit. I'm going home tomorrow, no matter what. The ankle will be fine."

SPENCER RUBBED HIS EYES, realizing it wasn't just his worst nightmare, it was his reality. She was going home. He was getting accustomed to having her here, seeing her every day. A part of him had hoped they could just go on like this, being together, but without all the pomp and circumstance and discussion of forever. For Spencer, tomorrow was much easier to contemplate than forever.

He nodded politely to Beth's grandmother. "Good evening, Mrs. Von Meeter."

"Mr. James," she drolled. "It is so nice to see you again."

"Spencer!" Joan exclaimed, panic in her eyes. "I was just leaving."

Thank God. "Why are you here?" he asked, as he walked her to the door.

"You've wanted to give up the alimony for four years, and I've come to grant your wish."

"Congratulations. Harry's a lucky man," said Spencer, smiling politely and hoping Harry had bought into the supplemental mental-health policy. He was going to need it.

After he saw Joan into the cab, he came back upstairs.

"You're here to see Beth?" he asked her grandmother, making polite conversation, and rather proud of himself for the effort.

"Actually, I was hoping to talk to you as well." She smiled at him, sitting perfectly still, but her eyes were sharp—razor sharp.

"Perfect," he lied. "Would you like to stay for dinner?"

"No, Mr. James, I have a reception at seven, so I'll be going shortly."

"Oh," he said, hoping he sounded disappointed.

"About my granddaughter."

Beth interrupted. "*Grand-mère,* there's no need for this conversation."

Muzzy focused on Beth. "You're living with this man. There is every need."

"We're not living together," clarified Beth. Spencer stayed quiet, glad that everyone had forgotten about him.

"Are you here?" asked Muzzy. "Is he here? You are both alive. I can see that for myself. Therefore, I will not tolerate this behavior."

Beth stood, winced, and then promptly sat down. "If I want to have a dog, if I want to live in sin, if I want to dance topless at a strip joint, I will. You cannot tell me what to do."

Muzzy turned back to Spencer. "Do you have something to say?"

And here it was. His big chance. His opportunity to tell Beth that he loved her, that he wanted to spend the rest of his life with her, that he didn't just want to live with her, he wanted to marry her.

Yet he said nothing. Instead he stared into the forbidding eyes of Muzzy Von Meeter, which seemed to lash away every layer of his cold existence, until there was nothing left.

He coughed. "Your granddaughter is a grown woman. She's done a fine job of living her own life. You should be proud of her. I think you're going to be late for your reception."

Muzzy met his eyes and stood. She had given him his opportunity and he had failed. They both knew it. "Beth, darling, retrieve my coat, will you?"

After Beth left the room, her grandmother addressed him one last time. "I had thought better of you, Mr. James."

Spencer didn't respond. For a short time, he had thought better of himself, as well.

"I'M GOING HOME TOMORROW." Beth stated unequivocally. There was no doubt in her voice, but her eyes waited for him to deny it.

"You'll be okay?" he asked.

"I'll be fine. If you'd like I can leave tonight," she said, staring down at the floor.

"No!" Then he realized how he sounded. "It's getting late. I'll drop you off at your place on my way into work. Do you have a date tonight?"

"No."

Yes. "Would you like to go out? Drinks or dinner?"

She frowned and stayed silent, just staring at the Christmas decorations she'd arranged.

Spencer swallowed hard. "We could go looking at Christmas lights," he said, knowing it was exactly the wrong thing to say, but he wanted to make her happy.

It was so easy to make her happy, and all he'd done was disappoint her. She smiled up at him. "You'd really go looking at Christmas lights? You don't mind?"

"Not a problem," he lied easily.

The first house was an eyesore, with a glow-in-the-dark manger and pink flamingos instead of camels. Spencer kept his mouth tightly shut.

After that, things got better as they drove by houses outlined in color. There were more stars out tonight than on Hollywood Boulevard. He caught himself smiling at one tasteful display of Santa climbing into a chimney. It wasn't a real smile, maybe just a crack of his lips, but he felt it just the same.

However, that was the last smile of the evening, and eventually he stopped trying, which was probably a better thing for both of them. He couldn't change the void inside him, even for her. But he sure wished that he could.

12

Sentimental SWF needs a man who can put stars in her eyes....

THE MORNING CAME FAR TOO early. Spencer awoke before her, and the smell of fresh coffee swirled in the dreams she had just before waking. She opened her eyes and remembered.

Today was the day she'd be leaving.

She slipped into the shower and washed her hair, her skin, bathing in the smell that surrounded him after a shower. As she was packing her toiletries, she slipped the half-used bar of soap into a plastic container. She pulled on her jeans and a heavy cotton sweater and applied her makeup more carefully than usual. Finally, she was ready. Calm, composed, sophisticated.

She practiced smiling in the mirror, and when she felt strong, she made her way to the bedroom.

When she saw him, the smile stuttered. He was half-dressed. Jeans, no shirt. Shower-damp hair that was more brown than gold. When he saw her, his gaze slid away.

There they were, two lovers seeing each other as strangers. *Folie à deux.*

Beth lifted her bag. "Got everything in here. I used the last of your soap, by the way. Sorry."

"Don't worry about it."

Beth watched with jealous eyes as he snagged a shirt from his closet and shrugged into it. She fisted her hands so her fingers wouldn't give her away.

All too soon he was driving her back home, where she belonged. Her own apartment. There would be no more playing house. And now it was time for goodbye. There was an art to a gracious goodbye. Courtesy followed with warmth. Today she felt neither courteous nor warm.

"You'll be okay?" he asked, and she wondered what he'd do if she said no. However, that was too close to making a scene, too telling.

Instead she nodded. "Thank you for your help," she murmured, her hands folded oh so correctly in front of her.

"Anytime. Call if you need anything," he said as he opened her apartment door.

"I'll be fine," Beth lied, smiling pertly.

"Do you want me to call you?" he asked, his gray eyes looking at her and looking through her, all at the same time. It was a particular talent that he had.

So this was it. If she told him to call, she knew exactly what would happen. They'd date, make love and her heart would be bound to him forever.

Sadly, his heart, or lack thereof, wouldn't be bound at all. It wasn't a life she could live.

"I don't think that's a good idea," she said.

For one short second, she saw the flicker of emotion on his face, first surprise, then pain, and finally admiration. "Ah, the truth. You're growing up, Beth."

"You taught me well," she answered, pleased that she wasn't crying.

"Take care of yourself. I'll stop by the tearoom."

"I can use all the customers I can get. Bring your friends."

"Okay," he agreed, unsmiling and dour, which was everything that she loved most about him. Then he left.

THE TEAROOM WAS THE perfect panacea. She couldn't stay in her empty apartment, so she picked up the morning paper and went to Printers Row.

As she walked through the doorway, she trailed approving fingers over the flocked scarlet wallpaper and the other furnishings. She was proud of what she'd done. The wooden chair rail was gleaming, freshly sanded and stained. The Persian carpets on the floor still smelled of new wool.

The tables and chairs sat empty now, but soon they would be full. She would see to that.

This was her place.

Bethany's.

A few short weeks ago, naming the tearoom after herself would have seemed arrogant. Now it seemed right.

She called the sign-makers office and left a message, punctuating the order with an arrogant "and rush it."

Still, there was much to do. She needed to get the menus printed and schedule the last of the city inspections. There must be hundreds of little things left to finish, but with two weeks left until opening day, it wasn't impossible anymore.

She picked up her toolbox and went to work, measuring the kitchen wall for the makeshift shelving she was going to put up.

Then her cell phone rang. Cassandra.

"You need to open your door. It's freezing outside."

"You're here?"

"Yes, I'm here. Now open the damn door."

Beth walked back into the serving area and unlocked the door.

"There."

Cassandra hung up. "Thank you. It's freezing out there. My nipples are about to break off."

"What are you here for?" Beth asked, as her friend hung up her coat on the rack.

Cassandra twirled, neatly attired in boot-cut jeans and a flannel shirt. The bourgeois effect was spoiled with the spiked-heel boots, but this was Cassandra, after all. "I'm here to work. However, let's deal with the important issues first. Caffeine?"

"Of course," said Beth, pouring a steaming cup of coffee.

"So what needs to be done?"

For three hours they worked together, putting up the remaining shelves, sweeping up the last of the construction dust, until Cassandra spied the paper sitting on the countertop and picked it up. "So how did the article read?"

Beth tested the handle on the walk-in, the refrigerated air not numbing her nearly as much as she would have liked. "I haven't read it yet. Stop loafing and get back to work."

"Why haven't you read it?" Cassandra asked, never having had a self-doubting moment in her life.

"It's times like these that I really hate you," explained Beth, slamming the heavy door.

Cassandra raised a brow. "Sore spot, aye?"

Beth scowled. "Yes." Then she picked up her tools and they walked into the main room.

"*I'm* going to read it," said Cassandra, sitting down and riffling through the pages until she found Spencer's article.

And that was why they all needed Cassandra. When push came to shove, Cassandra would do things without any fear of the consequences.

She began to read, and Beth's stomach pitted in anticipation. "What?"

Cassandra looked up and smiled. "Oh, this is good. Listen. 'When she talks about being lonely, she doesn't flinch or obscure the truth. The most basic of all needs is the need to find love. "I'm just going to search until I do." As she speaks, her eyes burn, focusing on places most people can't even see. Deep in her heart, she believes.'" Cassandra grinned. "He's got you pegged."

Beth tried to smile, but her mouth was staying stubborn.

"And wait, there's more." Cassandra took a sip of coffee. "'Each time she comes back from a date, the hope is still there. Another woman would have been discouraged or already have given up, but she keeps at it. To her it's as natural as breathing. As her friends get married, it doesn't dissuade her. If anything, she's only more committed to the path of true love. In a time when it's unfashionable for a woman to admit her yearning for companionship, she stands out from the crowd, picking her way through the soul-sucking tortures of dating in order to find it. Some people have no choice.'" Cassandra sighed. "I think I'm in love."

"Can I read it?"

"Sure." She handed over the paper, and Beth read through until she found the paragraph that she knew would be there. The answer to the question she hadn't dared ask.

"After her eighth date, she slows down, some of the enthusiasm gone. Her smile isn't as quick and the shadow of futility dodges her. 'He just doesn't seem real.' 'Boring.' 'Too focused.' She dismisses each one of her dates, except for one. Luck intervenes, or perhaps it's fate. Tall, handsome, with a charming smile, Michael is the logical counterpoint for Beth. She explains it best: 'When two people are meant to be together, they find a way.'"

Beth stopped reading, because there wasn't any reason to continue. It was a beautiful tribute, but the message was clear. He expected her to move on, with his blessing. She allowed herself one long sigh but no more. Then she looked over at Cassandra. "We don't have time for this."

She stood and walked into the kitchen, dropping the paper into the trash.

Wisely, Cassandra kept quiet.

THE NEXT DAY, Spencer was back pounding the streets. This time it wasn't city hall, it was Santa Claus. Not exactly hard news. Still, wasn't this his chance to find out if the milk of human kindness pulsed through him? This was a test. Not that he was optimistic, because he'd always failed in the past, so what made him think today would be any different?

Maybe. The Christmas tree, with the one small present underneath, was still sitting in his apartment, and he did think that yesterday's snow had melted away a little faster than normal.

Frank Capra he wasn't, but maybe there was enough inside him for her.

He started off at Daley Plaza where, nestled between the towering skyscrapers, a quaint German village sat.

Christkindlmarket was adorned with heavy kitsch and the merry sound of "ka-ching." The scene came complete with an eighty-five-foot-high holiday tree, currently bedecked with enough light-bulbs to illuminate the dark side of the moon. Spencer shook his head. Did people know Chicago had a budget crisis? Probably not.

Everywhere you looked frantic shoppers and screaming children pounded the streets. He wandered the booths, hands stuffed in his pockets, trying to understand the appeal of dust-gathering knickknacks, most of which had no functional purpose at all. Beth would love this explosion of capitalistic gluttony. Spencer just shook his head. The world was a sad, sad place.

His first appointment was with Santa himself. He went to Santa's House and approached the head elf.

"I'm here to see Santa," he said quietly.

"Excuse me?"

"Spencer James. *Chicago Herald.* I'm here to see Santa."

Three militant mothers glared. The elf raised up little green elf-glove-covered hands. "You'll have to get to the end of the line, sir."

But there was no freaking way that Spence was going to wait three hours behind Suzy Scream-a-Lot and Tommy the Tasmanian Tornado in order to get his interview. "I have an appointment. Eleven-thirty."

The elf checked her watch, her large pointy ears bobbing. "Santa's going to lunch at noon."

The little girl in front of him began to cry. "I'm not going to see Santa?" she wailed.

Her mother hugged her close and shot Spencer a look of disgust. "Of course you are, Madison."

Spencer felt it necessary to defend his character. "Santa was excited about talking to the *Herald,* you know. A chance to tell all the good people of Chicago about Christmas spirit, goodwill, love and—" Spencer struggled for a minute and then snapped his fingers "—oh, yeah, and peace."

The elf frowned, but disappeared, presumably to ask Santa if he was amenable. After a few minutes, she returned. "He'll see you promptly at noon."

Madison began to cry even louder. The elf's ears bobbed again as she crouched down to pat the little girl. "It's all right, Santa is still going to see you, too."

"And how is Santa going to be in two places at one time?" Spencer growled, not really wanting to interview Santa with a five-year-old girl on his lap.

"We have two Santas," whispered the elf, nodding her head in Madison's direction. "Now if you could move aside..."

Politely Spencer stepped to the back of the room and took out his cell phone, anxious to get some real work done. While he was setting up a meeting with a policy consultant for a national political party, some kid began to bawl.

"Can you hold on a minute?" Spencer asked, and then proceeded to remedy the problem. He turned to the mother—and wasn't it always the mother with problem children? "Excuse me, I'm trying to talk on the phone. Can you work with your daughter to get her quiet?"

The mother glared. "This is my son."

Spencer noted the child again. "Okay, can you work with your son to get him quiet, then?"

"Mister, we've been waiting for forty-five minutes to see Santa and Robby's tired. This is his nap time."

Well, why are you here? he wanted to ask. However, he held his tongue. "Does he draw?" Spencer asked.

At the mom's nod, he pulled out his extra Uniball pen and gave the little monster a piece of paper. And then proceeded to get back to work.

Finally, it was his time to see Santa. The head elf led him to a small room in the back. There was Santa, big, round, red, just like in all the commercials.

"Ho, ho, ho," he said.

Spencer smiled politely. "It's all right, you can be normal now."

Santa stroked his beard. "Spencer James, the reporter?"

"Yes, I have a few questions for you, so if you don't mind, I'll just take some notes while we talk." He flipped open his notebook. "First off, what is your real name?"

Santa looked offended. "Santa Claus."

Spencer smiled tightly. "Yeah, I know that's what you tell all the kiddies, but that's not the focus here. Our readers are *adults.* I'm just writing about what it takes to be Santa Claus and why you do it."

"I have no choice."

Spencer tapped his pen on the paper. This was getting nowhere. "Okay, we'll just call you the Santa that prefers to be anonymous. Bet it's contractual."

Santa just looked peeved. "Next question?"

"Well, what do you do the other eleven months of the year, although I guess it's only ten, now that they're starting Christmas the day after Halloween."

"You can say that I'm 'retired' when I'm not being

Santa. I think both your readers and I will be happy with that answer."

Spencer scribbled his notes down on the pad. "Okay, I need something else to write here, since we're not going to get much in the way of Santa's personal life. Do you have a heartwarming anecdote, a sick kid story or something?"

For the next thirty minutes, Santa overloaded Spencer with schmaltz. A more sensitive man would have been reduced to tears. It was good stuff for the paper, but Spencer was unmoved.

He folded up his pad and held out his hand to Santa. "Thanks for cooperating."

"You don't have any Christmas wishes?"

Spencer shook his head. "I'm too old for that."

Santa started to laugh. "You think you're too *old*? Humor an old man trying to do his job. I won't tell."

Oh, yeah. This was good. The old guy needed to keep up the act. "I don't think Santa can put this under my Christmas tree," he said with a wink.

Santa peered at Spencer over the wire rims of his spectacles. "A skeptic, hmm?"

"I don't believe in anything. I'm a journalist."

"So when will you run the story?"

"You can read it on Christmas Day."

Santa laughed. "I'll read it the next day. I'm busy on Christmas."

Spencer just nodded appropriately and headed

for the door. The old guy had watched *Miracle on 34th Street* one too many times.

"Oh, and Spencer," Santa called.

Spencer turned and looked.

"Don't forget to check under your tree Christmas Eve."

"I thought you came on Christmas."

"For you, I'm making an exception."

Spencer waved his pen at Santa. *Right.*

SPENCER'S NEXT STOP WAS a soup kitchen on North Avenue. This was new territory for him. When he stepped through the door he immediately knew why he'd never been in one before. The place was packed with bums, all waiting in line for food. Male bums, female bums; obviously homelessness was equal-opportunity. Spencer moved to the front of the line and was promptly shoved to the back.

"You can't cut in," an ageless creature declared.

By this time, Spencer knew the drill. "I'm not here to eat, I just want to talk to the people who operate this place."

"You can wait until after I eat," the creature snarled.

Not liking the feral gleam in the man's eyes, Spencer decided to wait. So he settled at the back of the room and watched the dynamics of a soup kitchen in action. Most of the bums were loners, not talking to anyone, eyes looking ahead or down at their feet.

Some were talking to themselves, singing, laughing, or even in one case, yelling.

Spencer took out his pad and started to write, wondering about the stories of all these people who were going to spend Christmas alone. Suddenly "alone" didn't seem right anymore. He tapped an older woman on the shoulder.

"Excuse me. I'm a reporter from the *Chicago Herald*. Do you mind if I ask you a few questions?"

She ignored him.

He tried again. Finally, the man next to her spoke up. "I'll talk to you."

Spencer moved over to the empty chair next to him. "How long have you been out of a job?"

"Pretty much all my life."

"How did you find out about this place?"

"Word gets around. The food's pretty bad, but it's warm."

"Got any plans for Christmas?"

"When's that?"

"Next Tuesday."

He poked at the green vegetable concoction on his plate with the plastic fork. "Nope. Don't think so. Tuesday nights I usually go to St. Francis for dinner. I'll be there."

Spencer realized he didn't have plans for Christmas, either. Maybe St. Francis took in the non-homeless as well. "If you could have one thing for

Christmas, what would it be?" he asked, proud of himself for thinking up such a sensitive question.

"I think I'd like a dog."

"You wouldn't want a million dollars, maybe a mansion on the Gold Coast?"

"Nope. A dog."

Spencer was curious. "Why would you want a dog when you could have anything in the world?"

"I think I should have something to take care of. I'm not up to taking care of a person, but I think I could manage a dog."

Spencer stared into the swirls of processed meat and vegetables laced with food coloring and waited for the pulse of emotion to beat through him. It was touching, unselfish, everything that a human being should appreciate.

Nothing.

And that seemed to sum it up nicely. When it came to humanity, he was deficient. He'd done all this work just to prove to himself that a relationship between Bo Peep and the abominable snowman wasn't insane. No, the only thing insane was a grown man scrounging about the city during the week before Christmas in search of his heart.

He went to talk to the director of the soup kitchen, spent twenty minutes arguing with the man about whether the current facility layout was operationally sound. Any fool could see that if they moved the line to form on both sides of the table, they could feed people more quickly. Finally, Spencer ended up getting thrown out.

Outside, the Salvation Army volunteer was ringing his bell, shouting "Merry Christmas," and Spencer swore at him. The sound of the ringing bell was deafening. More to the desire to stop the ringing than anything else, Spence took out his wallet and stuffed three twenties in the kettle.

The man started to smile. "Thank you."

Spencer put his hands in his pockets and wondered what was wrong with him. That one night when he'd looked at Christmas lights with her, he was sure he'd felt something. Some mass of tissue inside that contained something more than vessels and veins. He kept waiting, hoping it would grow, but every day he just felt colder than the day before.

He pulled his coat tight around him and buried his face in the collar. The afternoon wind was starting to blow and snowflakes were whirling in the gray skies. All around him, people hurried to get to their destinations, their faces reddened from the gusts.

Spence felt like laughing. They all thought the temperature was cold outside, but compared to the frozen wasteland inside him, everything else was balmy.

13

SWF is too busy to look for a man right now. Check back after the holidays....

TWO DAYS BEFORE CHRISTMAS, Beth was training the new waiters. The last three to be hired were Thomas, Seth and Charles, and they needed the most help.

The trio was a handsome bunch, bless their little hearts, but they didn't have a lot going on upstairs. She was helping them fill in their W-4's when her grandmother arrived. Now this was a surprise. Muzzy looked elegant, as always, in a long woolen coat with a mink collar, her white hair perfectly done.

She spied Thomas, Seth and Charles, and one white crescent eyebrow arched high into the fabled Von Meeter forehead. "Bethany, I think we need to discuss something. Boys, could we have a moment alone?"

When they were alone, her grandmother started in. "This isn't the image that I think the tearoom should have."

Beth was ready for that one. "Don't worry. I'm putting them in tuxedos, not G-strings."

"But it's beefcake. It's too...tawdry."

"Exactly. We'll make a fortune, *Grand-mère*. Everyone needs a gimmick. Ours is hot guys."

Her grandmother took off her coat. "I don't like it."

Beth kicked her feet up on a chair, her ankle now almost its normal size. "You hired me to run this joint."

"It's a tearoom, not a joint."

"Okay, you hired me to run this tearoom. You're going to have to let me do this my way, or else the deal is off."

"Don't get all bothered, Bethany."

In the past, the remark would have been enough to make her back down. Not anymore. "I'm not bothered. I'm being assertive."

"Yes, my dear, I realize that. Now, back to business. The furnishings. Very nice. I approve."

Faint praise, but it was a start. "Thank you."

"But are you sure about those...boys?"

Beth nodded. "Oh, yes. You're going to be the talk of the town, *Grand-mère*."

"That's not *exactly* what I had in mind."

"You wanted me to find my path. I have." She crossed her arms across her chest. Resolute. Steadfast. Rock-solid.

"I'm sorry about your young man."

"I'm sorry, too."

Her grandmother reached out and gave her a quick hug. Nothing too long that might muss the hair.

Thomas came out of the back. "Miss Von Meeter, your phone is ringing."

When he spied her grandmother working to put on her coat, he sprang into action, just as Bethany had taught the waiters.

"Let me help you."

Her grandmother's lip curled up, her eyelashes fluttering in what some might term a flirtatious manner. "Thank you, young man."

"Call me Thomas, ma'am."

"And you must call me Muzzy."

Her grandmother walked out the door, but with a kick in her step that hadn't been there before. She turned to Beth and winked. "Maybe you're right, after all."

ON SUNDAY NIGHT, Spencer ended up at city hall. It was ghostlike with only a few harried workers walking the halls. It was Spence's habit to show up there, get caught up in the hum of politics and see who was meeting with whom when they shouldn't.

Spencer spied one lonely security guard. "Evening, Frank."

"Evening, Spencer. You should be at home."

Spencer shook his head. He didn't want to be

home. "Anything going on tonight, Frank?" Security guards made great anonymous sources.

"Noah Barclay was here earlier, meeting with the city planners. That's been about it." The old man checked his watch. "I'm leaving at eleven. Going home. Got presents to wrap. It's twelve degrees outside. A sane man would be warming his toes by the fire, preferably with his woman and his remote control at his side."

"Nothing decent on television but the news," said Spencer, ignoring the sharp stab of pain he felt. Surely it would go away in time. The little Christmas tree was starting to get to him, and he'd almost thrown it in the trash. But when it came time to tossing it, he couldn't.

"Call Barclay. He'll talk. He's fishing about for the transportation contract. Trust me. A man spends seventeen years around these halls and he gets to know what's what."

Spencer smiled. That was exactly what he needed. He called Noah and arranged to meet him at a bar over on Milwaukee Avenue.

Work was the perfect solution, certainly more forgiving than alcohol. Articles on Santa Claus and Internet love just weren't cutting it. This was Spence's chance to get back into real work. Get back into his real life.

When he entered the bar, it was quiet and empty.

The bartender was polishing the brass railing, humming "Jingle Bells" under his breath.

No sign of Noah at all. Wonderful.

Spence pulled out his PDA and went through the records of his expenses. It wasn't his favorite exercise, but it was better than sitting alone, staring into an ever-diminishing glass of scotch.

Finally, his former brother-in-law appeared.

"Thanks for coming," said Spencer.

"That's okay. You sounded...anxious."

Anxious wasn't good. Spencer took a deep breath. "Let's talk about work. Your company. Anvil. The city's highway and transportation project. Are you going to bid on it?"

"No comment. Off the record, I've got contractors to hire and suppliers to negotiate with. It's a long way away. Moving a company across the world isn't easy, and the city isn't close to having a firm proposal. Talk to me in six months and we'll know if it'll be viable."

They talked for a little longer, Spencer filling Noah in on the city scandals. "Be glad you missed it all. They're cracking down. That's why they hired O'Malley."

"Yeah, I met him," said Noah, not looking enthused.

"You'll have to get past him."

"I can."

"Okay, this is good. We can run an article after

the first of the year," said Spencer, making notes. This was work. This was news. This felt right.

Noah shook his head. "No article. It's too soon. And besides, tomorrow is Christmas Eve. Stop with the work already." He took a sip of his drink. "Are you going home for the holidays?"

Spencer frowned. "I am home."

"Oh...what are you going to do tomorrow?"

"Sleep late, maybe watch a little TV." Spencer smiled, trying to convince him that would be fun.

"You could come over—oh, bad idea."

All the holiday talk was getting to be too much for Spencer. Slowly, he put away his notebook. He had to admit to himself that work hadn't fixed anything. Finishing his scotch, he asked, "How was being away?"

"Okay, but not great."

"Happy to be back, huh?"

"Oh, yeah. I never truly appreciated American women until I was home again."

Spencer nodded in what he thought would be a traditional guy way. "Sure."

There was a long, awkward silence, and finally Noah sighed.

"Spencer, why am I here?"

"I needed a friend."

Noah arched a brow. "Does this have to do with Joan?"

Spencer shook his head.

"Do you want to talk?"

Spencer shook his head.

"Do you want to drink?"

Spencer thought for a minute. Drinking seemed to be the easiest way to forget the void in his heart. He had thought that was just who he was. Now he was wondering if maybe the piece of his heart that was missing was Beth. "Drinking would be good."

Noah ordered two doubles. "Are you a scotch man?" asked Spencer, now realizing he underappreciated his former brother-in-law.

"No, these are for you. I think one of us is going to have to stay sober, and I *don't* think it's going to be you."

MICHAEL SHOWED UP at Beth's apartment on Christmas Eve's eve. She had thought about not answering the door, but that was the coward's way out.

He had champagne—one point—strawberries—one point—and a calorie-free pot of poinsettias.

Not only romantic, but practical as well. They ended up watching a movie on the couch, an old classic that Beth would normally have loved. But tonight she spent the evening critiquing her own stupid choices in men.

"Beth, I get the feeling that something's not working here. No offense, but I've pretty much tried everything to get you to take notice, but I feel like you're just not paying attention."

"That's not true," said Beth automatically, even as she mentally rapped her knuckles for lying. Maybe she hadn't paid attention until now, but she could. She would. Here was a man who was kind, sensitive, and genuinely understood the mechanics of a relationship. What the hell was she thinking?

Beth stared up at him. *I think I can. I think I can. I think I can.*

And he lowered his head for the kiss.

14

SWF looking for Mr. Perfect. All UnPerfects need not apply....

CHRISTMAS EVE STARTED badly for Spencer. First, he was hungover. Second, his notes from last evening were nothing more than a blur of black ink and the smell of old scotch. And the kicker, the piece that he hated most, he discovered when he looked into the mirror.

He'd gotten a tattoo.

He had a vague recollection of walking home through the cold, dark streets of the city. A moon-struck man shouldn't be left alone. He could end up in an uptown tattoo parlor doing the unthinkable.

But there was no denying the proof. And it was a miserable thing. A heart, with a ribbon across it saying Beth. And did he get it someplace discreet like on his back, or his butt? Oh, no, it was on his chest, right above his heart. And right now it hurt. He stepped into the shower and scratched and scrubbed, thinking that he'd been smart and just gotten a temporary one.

Soon, his skin was raw, his soap was gone, and he realized the awful truth. He'd gotten a permanent tattoo.

Christ.

He spent the rest of the morning sitting on his bed, staring into the mirror, a freaking headache throbbing in the middle of his forehead and an itchy heartache in his chest.

When he turned on CNN, to find out what mayhem was ruining the world, they didn't have news, they had fluff. Everywhere he looked he was surrounded by fluff. Didn't real news happen at Christmas? Obviously not.

The elections weren't over, and were they covering that? No. Somewhere in Africa, children were starving, but was anyone paying attention? No. They were all too busy worrying about last-minute gifts.

Then he spied the small tree that he'd relegated to the corner. And the little package underneath. Carefully, he unwrapped the paper. Presents had never been a big tradition in his family. In fact, Christmas hadn't been a big tradition, either, so he made the unwrapping last as long as he could.

Eventually a small white box emerged. He opened the lid and inside was a red Uniball pen. He frowned to himself. Very practical, very mundane and very disappointing.

So what had he been expecting? He was ready to

put it back under the tree when he noticed a small white piece of paper, hidden under the pen.

He pulled it out and opened up the note. There, inked in red Uniball ink, was a tiny red heart, complete with elaborate red flourishes.

Slowly he sank into a chair, his eyes tracing over the thin red lines, memorizing the tiny shape. For a long time he sat there, astounded by the power of an insignificant little drawing.

There was his future—laid out on a small piece of paper, in red Uniball ink. He raced to his closet and pulled on a sweater and jeans, determined to do what he should have done the first moment he saw her. He had tried so hard to resist the irresistible, but not anymore.

Unfortunately, now he had to find the perfect gift for her, and giving really wasn't his forte.

He started downtown, but the streets were only filled with last-minute shoppers trudging through the snow. The Chicago Board of Trade was deserted. The early morning traders were long gone, no doubt sitting in front of warm fires with their significant others.

Such a telling phrase, "significant other." Spencer rubbed his heart, the wool sweater aggravating the itch. Damn thing.

"Hey, bud. Anything happening here?" He laid down two quarters for a copy of the *Sun-Times*, noticing the last-minute gift guide that was advertised on the front page.

"Nope."

Then out of the corner of his eye, Spencer spied the magazine. The December issue of *True Fantasies.* Maybe it was fate, after all. He began to smile and picked up the top copy. "How much for this one?"

"Four ninety-five."

"Four ninety-five? It's a piece of garbage."

"Look, bub, you want the piece of garbage or not?"

Spencer dug through his pockets, coming up with a five. "Keep the change."

"Hey, Merry Christmas," the man said as Spencer walked away.

He passed the Salvation Army volunteer, an older woman with short blond hair, who reminded him of Beth. He stopped. It was her smile. It was below freezing, the wind was starting to kick up the snow and the woman was ringing a bell. Still, she was smiling.

He began to smile, too.

Again, he fished around in his pockets, proud to come up with a twenty. He stuffed it in the black kettle and the old lady nodded. "Merry Christmas."

"Yeah, whatever," he said, but his feet were moving faster now, his breath visible in the chilled air. A sound came from him, almost unrecognizable. Yeah, that was it. It was laughter.

So FAR, Beth had seen pretty much the whole run of Christmas movies and she wasn't feeling any merrier. *A Christmas Carol*. Eh? *It's a Wonderful Life*. And didn't she know how that felt? *How the Grinch Stole Christmas*. The Whos were suckers.

In fact, she had pretty much convinced herself that it didn't matter if it was Christmas Eve. Today she was going down to the tearoom to do something. *Anything*. Reorganize the dishes. Test out the new recipe she'd found for crème brûlée. This year she didn't feel merry at all.

She put on her coat and scarf and was just walking out of her apartment building when she saw him coming up the sidewalk. At first she wasn't sure. Maybe her eyes were failing her? And then he got closer. The frown looked familiar, even with the snow dusting that dark gold hair. There was only one man who could scowl like that.

Spencer. She forgot her resolution to be strong and cool and controlled, although she didn't launch herself into his arms.

"What is this?" he asked, opening up the magazine and stabbing his finger at the page. Obviously "hello" was a forgotten piece of his vocabulary.

"You found my story," she said, pleased that he'd actually bought the tabloid.

"Who is this pool boy?"

She began to smile. "You need to come upstairs. It's sixteen degrees with a windchill factor of three."

"I thought you loved winter," he said cautiously.

"Among other things," she said, catching his arm and leading him into the building.

He gave her a sharp look, but she kept quiet.

Quickly she unlocked her door before he could change his mind.

After they were inside her apartment, he stood, looking out of place and uncomfortable, his coat still on, even his gloves.

"Is this a short visit?" she asked, sitting on the couch, sounding more sure of herself than she felt.

"There are things I need to say."

"I'm assuming you'll be honest, then," she said, her heart starting to beat once more.

"Of course. I'm a journalist." He took off his gloves and searched in his pocket until he found his pen, which he began to roll between his fingers. "First of all, I don't believe in Santa Claus."

Oh, he was hating this, she thought, starting to smile. "I don't either," she lied, although she *was* starting to believe in miracles.

"Second of all, I don't sing. I will never sing."

"Ever?" she asked.

"Never," he said firmly.

"That's all right then. I have an aversion to singing." An aversion she'd developed three seconds after trying to kiss her way into a relationship that she knew was doomed to failure.

"What else?" she asked.

"I don't know," he said, his eyes scanning her apartment, looking everywhere but at her.

"Why are you here?" Beth asked, with a sigh.

Another woman might have run from the fierce look on his face, but she was tougher than that now. "Because I don't have a choice."

"You don't look thrilled," she said, practicing his journalistic style of honesty.

"I'm scared," he admitted, the pen in his hand beginning to twirl.

"Of what?"

"But I have to try."

"Try what?"

"I'm not going to make any promises—well, no, that's wrong. I will make a promise to you. I'm going to love you forever, I know that now. But I'm not sure that you're going to love me that long. I think you think you do today, but you don't know me. You could end up hating me...or something. I'm not a nice person."

He was still wearing his coat, the pen circling faster now, every defense kicked into overdrive.

He needed her, and the terms didn't matter anymore. "A porcupine has less needles, but I love you...even with the needles. I've seen the worst of you, Spencer James. You don't scare me."

"It can always get worse," he muttered.

She could live with anything now. "It's not like we'll be seeing each other every day. When you get tired of me, you can go home," she said quietly, but the words still echoed in the room.

"No, we're going to do this right."

Her spirits notched up an inch. "You want to cohabitate?"

"Yes."

She thought long and hard. It wasn't perfect. Her family would be scandalized, but they'd get over it. And if it was the only way she could have him, so be it. "All right, but we have to find a new apartment." She wanted a new beginning. A place of their own.

"That seems fair."

"Are you going to stay?" she asked calmly.

"Yes."

"Shouldn't you take off your coat, then?"

Another scowl. "You're enjoying this, aren't you?"

"Immensely," she said, with a satisfied smile.

He took off his coat and laid it across the chair. He went and sat down next to her on the couch. Still he didn't try and touch her, and she wasn't going to make the first move. It was all up to him.

"What is it?" she asked, trying to figure out what was left to cover.

"I have your present," he said, and he pulled out a small box, no wrapping paper. "I got it for you today."

It wasn't a ring box; it was too big for that. "I should wait until tomorrow."

"Don't you dare," he said.

Carefully she lifted the lid and peeked inside. It was the most god-awful pin she'd ever seen. About four inches high, bigger than her entire breast. It was a Christmas tree covered in what looked to be tiny deer. Then she read the little banner above it. Merry Christmoose.

"Why are you giving me this?" she asked, wondering if this was some new, obscure method to drive her away.

"Because I wanted you to have something that I would never in a million years buy. It took every bit of courage to buy this pin, and I almost returned it three times."

"That's because it's butt-ugly."

"I know," he said, almost proudly. "That's what Christmas is all about. When you dig through all the tackiness, and ugliness, and vile shoppers, it's just about a day that you spend making the people you love happy. If I could reduce myself to buying something like this, it would make you happy."

Oh, they had a long way to go. "You do make me happy," she said, and she realized it was true.

"Will you do something for me?"

"What?"

"Marry me, please."

She froze, waiting for the punch line, for the retraction, for any signal at all that this was a very bad joke. But he looked dead serious. He stared into her eyes, and her breathing slowed to a stop.

"Why?" she asked, because this was important.

"Because I'm better with you than I am without you. I need you if I'm ever going to make this human thing work."

"I thought you were happy the way you were."

He shrugged. "That's the problem with being arrogant. You miss these things. At one time, I think I was. But now I'm not."

"And I make you happy?" she asked, amazed at the power he'd just handed her.

"You will in about three seconds, if you'll tell me yes. Don't make me wait any longer."

When he looked as vulnerable as this, she couldn't deny him anything, much less her heart. "Yes."

He exhaled. "Oh, thank God." Then he looked at her carefully. "I love you, you know?"

"I know," she said, and kissed him. "I love you, too," she whispered when she came up for air. "I almost made a bad mistake."

"You could still be making a bad mistake," he said, brushing the hair from her face.

She shook her head. "I don't think so. I need you. When I'm with you, I can be truthful—" she punctuated it with a kiss "—arrogant—" she climbed into his lap "—and demanding," she said as she began to unbutton his shirt.

He covered her hands in his. "Let's turn out the lights first."

She shook her head. "Oh, no. Broad daylight. Face-to-face."

"But—" he started and she shushed him with a finger to his lips.

"No buts. Remember, demanding."

Slowly she began to unbutton his shirt, one button, two, and then she spied it. "Oh my God."

He winced. "I got a tattoo."

Epilogue

Forget it.

SOMEONE WAS AT HER DOOR when Beth awoke the next morning. She rolled over and found Spencer, a smile growing on her face. Lazily he pulled her close, limbs mingling, bare flesh brushing against bare flesh. He was burying his lips in her neck when the knocking sounded again.

She pulled on her robe and went to see who it was.

The living room was light and cheery, with sunshine spilling in through the curtains, and she realized it was later than she had first thought.

As she opened the door, singing began. A fairly good version of "Jingle Bells" came back at her, but it wasn't the Mormon Tabernacle Choir.

It was Jessica, Adam, Mickey, Dominic, and yes, even Cassandra.

Jessica spoke first. "We came early. Wanted to get in before you headed out to see your family. Nobody needs to spend Christmas morning alone. And we brought presents, too," she said, barging into the living room.

"That's so sweet," said Beth, fighting back tears.

Cassandra stepped forward, dazzling in a tight black sweater, and put a red-wrapped package in her hand. "I know it's tough now, but you'll do fine. It's really not that hard. This is for you. It's not a vibrator, but I did consider it."

Beth wiped her eyes. "Oh, you guys are the best."

"How's the foot?" asked Mickey.

"Good as new," she said, showing off her newly trim ankle.

Jessica came up and hugged her. "We were worried about you," she whispered in her ear.

"You don't have to be," Beth whispered back.

"We're friends. We do that."

And then Spencer came out and the silence was deafening. He had put on his shirt, jeans and shoes, but well, it wasn't hard to put two and two together.

Cassandra arched her brow. "Mr. James, what a surprise."

Spencer came and stood next to Beth, speaking out of the corner of his mouth. "You have a lot of friends."

Beth smiled and whispered back, "Get used to it."

He nodded seriously. "Okay."

"That was a joke."

"Right. I knew that."

Mickey frowned. "Is this a good thing? I think this is a bad thing."

Spencer stepped forward and took a deep breath.

"I love her, I want to spend forever with her. I don't just want to live with her, I want to marry her." Then he exhaled and smiled. "I did it. I said it. I did it."

His eyes met hers, and Beth curled an arm around him. "I *love* this man." Now she had more than she had ever dreamed possible.

Jessica immediately launched herself at Spencer and caught him in a big hug. "I can't believe this. This is so great."

Cassandra sat down in the chair. "Is anyone surprised? I said this was going to happen. I told her so, but did she listen? *No. Not gonna happen.* Bachelorette Pact? What's that?"

Mickey hit Cassandra on the shoulder to shut her up.

Beth looked at Spencer and lost herself in the warm gray of his eyes. He bent his head and kissed her. And they never noticed when everyone left.

* * * * *

Don't miss Cassandra—the last bachelorette—
and her story in Temptation 979
THE LONGEST NIGHT
coming next month!

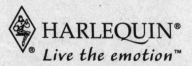

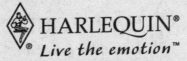

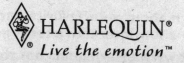

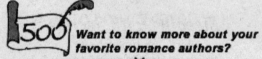

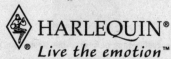